THE IMPOSSIBLE GROOM

JENNIFER YOUNGBLOOD

GET YOUR FREE BOOK

Get Beastly Charm: A Contemporary retelling of beauty & the beast as a welcome gift when you sign up for my newsletter. You'll get information on my new releases, book recommendations, discounts, and other freebies.

Get the book at:

http://bit.ly/freebookjenniferyoungblood

1

Something was up. Ryleigh could tell from the looks passing between Tess and her client Gemma. "What am I missing?" When neither of them answered, she zeroed in on her younger sister. "Tess, what's going on?"

Tess's eyes gleamed with excitement as she clasped her hands together and leaned forward across the kitchen table where they were sitting. "I did something." A sheepish expression cloaked her face.

Ryleigh tensed. Tess was as free-spirited as Ryleigh was sensible. Over the past few years, as Ryleigh had worked to get her business up and running, Tess had proved invaluable. Still, she enjoyed pushing the envelope. There was no telling what she'd done this time. "Will one of you please tell me what's going on?" Ryleigh demanded, not trying to hide the exasperation in her voice.

A large smile filled Gemma's round face, the wrinkles around her eyes deepening. "We're so proud of you," she cooed.

"Proud of me for what?"

"You've been selected for the Grilling and Chilling Cooking Competition," Tess exploded with glee.

Ryleigh's head did a one-eighty spin. "What?" she swallowed, trying to take it all in. The competition was huge! In a month, professional chefs from all over the country would gather at the convention center in downtown Dallas to compete for a $15K prize. The publicity alone would boost Ryleigh's business as a personal chef. She'd desperately wanted to enter the contest, but the entry fee was fifteen hundred dollars. Ryleigh nixed the idea knowing that hundreds of people would enter, but only ten would be chosen to compete. No way could Ryleigh throw away fifteen hundred dollars on a pipe dream. She shot Tess an accusing look. "You went behind my back and signed me up."

Tess arched an eyebrow. "Yes, I did. You can thank me later," she added tartly.

Ryleigh let out a long breath. "Where did you get the entry money?" The look on Gemma's face instantly answered her question. "You paid the entry fee." Gemma and her husband Doug were Ryleigh's best clients. For the past year, she'd been coming to their home on a weekly basis to prepare meals. The retired couple had become close friends with Ryleigh and Tess, to the point where the sisters felt closer to them than they ever had to their own parents. Still, Tess shouldn't have taken advantage of Gemma's generosity.

"Yes," Gemma admitted. "I knew it would be money well spent and that you'd make the cut." She chuckled, touching her stomach. "After all, I know firsthand how wonderful your cooking is."

Ryleigh clenched her fist, an invisible cord tightening around her chest. "What if I hadn't made it? You would've thrown away fifteen hundred dollars." Gemma's money might still go to waste. Ryleigh would be competing against top chefs from all over the US. Could she handle the pressure? She felt hot and cold at the same time.

Gemma lifted her chin, a sure note coming into her voice. "That was a chance I was willing to take."

Tess's brows drew together, her lips forming a pout. "Why're you being such a sour puss? You should be jumping for joy right now. Gemma and I did you a huge favor."

"You should've told me what you were doing," Ryleigh grumbled, "instead of going behind my back."

Sparks shot from Tess's eyes. "If we had, you would've put a monkey wrench in the whole thing like you always do." Her expression grew pleading. "You work so hard. You deserve a break. Don't let your fear of failure choke out your opportunity for success." She clutched her neck, gagging.

"I get the point," Ryleigh countered.

Tess's voice grew intense. "You can do this!"

"Yes," Gemma piped in, "Tess is right. You've got this, Ryleigh."

The air crackled with unleashed opportunity. Ryleigh drew in a breath. Was Tess right? Was she afraid of success? Things had been hard for her and Tess growing up. Their mom had left on a quest "to find herself" when Ryleigh was ten, leaving their father a broken-down and bitter man, who had no idea how to raise two daughters. Consequently, Ryleigh and Tess had raised themselves. Then Ryleigh got married to the man she thought would be the love of her life, only to have the relationship end in divorce. She'd become jaded, never allowing herself to get too hopeful about the future. She had to keep her feet firmly planted in the present so she could provide a good home for Noah. Her heart softened as she glanced to the adjoining family room where her seven-year-old son was sprawled out on the floor, watching TV. Despite the pain she'd experienced over her failed relationship with her ex-husband Joey, Ryleigh was intensely grateful for her young son.

Ryleigh was an official participant in the contest. She'd made the cut! Her stomach tingled with anticipation as a smile tugged at her lips. She looked at Tess and Gemma. She needed to think more positively, stop being so afraid of the sky falling all the time. "Do you really think I can do it?"

Tess pounded the table with the flat of her palm. "Absolutely!"

Everything began to sink in, as Ryleigh's eyes glistened. "I can't believe I was selected." Her head spun with possibilities. "What should I make?"

Gemma tucked a lock of silver hair behind her ear. "I vote for your peanut butter pie."

Ryleigh wrinkled her nose. "Do you think it's sophisticated enough?"

"You can dress it up a little." Tess waved a hand. "Put a gourmet spin on it."

"Yes, I could." Ryleigh bit her lower lip, thinking. "For the grill part ... should I do fish? Or beef or chicken?"

Tess flicked her fingers through her hair. "Fish is your specialty. Then again, we are in Texas so beef is always a good choice." She shrugged. "It's up to you. You're the chef."

"Hmm ... I'll have to think about it," Ryleigh mused, drumming her fingers on the table.

"The wheels are already turning," Gemma laughed.

Noah bounded into the kitchen and tugged on Ryleigh's t-shirt sleeve. "Can we go to the park now?" He peered at her with big, brown eyes ringed in thick, dark lashes. "Please," he chimed.

Ryleigh ruffled his hair as she scooted back her chair and stood. "Yep. To the park we go."

"Yes!" Noah pumped a fist in the air and started jumping up and down.

Giving him an indulgent smile, Ryleigh put a hand on his shoulder. "All right. Take it down a notch." She looked apologetically at Gemma. "You'll be glad to get us out of here, so you can have some peace and quiet."

The corners of Gemma's lips turned down as she stood and brushed aside the comment with a wave of her hand. "Oh, no. I love having y'all here." She grinned at Noah. "This one, here, keeps me young."

Earlier, while Ryleigh worked on preparing freezer meals for Gemma, Tess had picked up Noah from school and brought him here to Gemma's house so they could finish up for the day. After downing a half dozen cookies and two glasses of milk, Noah started running circles around the kitchen, demanding Ryleigh's attention. Needing a diversion for Noah, Gemma had turned on the TV to one of Noah's favorite cartoons. Ryleigh promised to take Noah to the park, if he'd entertain himself long enough for them to finish up.

"Tess, do you want to come with us to the park?" Ryleigh asked.

Tess flipped the ends of her long, brown hair, hazel eyes sparkling. "I would, but I have a hot date."

A grin slid over Ryleigh's lips as she winked at Gemma. "Who's the lucky guy tonight?" Tess went out on so many dates that Ryleigh couldn't keep track of them all.

"His name's Marshall."

Gemma flashed a large smile. "Speaking of guys, I spoke to my neighbor about you the other day."

For a split second, Ryleigh thought Gemma was talking to Tess before realizing she was referring to her instead. She swallowed, pointing to herself. "Me?"

"Yep." Gemma's light, watery eyes shimmered beneath her wire-rimmed glasses. "Chas said he'd love to meet you."

Tess pumped her eyebrows in amusement. "Way to go, Gemma. Ryleigh needs to get out, let her hair down a little."

"Yeah, with Noah, I don't really have time to date," Ryleigh hedged.

Gemma waved her hand. "Nonsense. Douglas and I'll watch Noah while you go out."

Heat crawled up Ryleigh's neck, and she felt like she was pinned to the wall. "I don't think so."

"We'll get pizza and go see a movie," Gemma added, looking at Noah. "You'd like that, wouldn't you?"

"Mom! I wanna go with Gemma and Doug," Noah chimed. "Tonight?" he asked eagerly.

Gemma brought a finger to her chin, looking thoughtful. "I guess I could call Chas and see if he's available."

"No!" Ryleigh blurted. *Geez.* She felt like a charity case. She straightened to her full height. "I don't wish to be fixed up with anyone right now," she said stiffly.

"Oh, Chas O'Brien's not just anyone," Gemma said. "He's a cutie and the starting running back for the Texas Titans. The Irish Flash is what they're calling him because he's so quick on the field. Chas recently broke up with his girlfriend. Right now, he's footloose and fancy free. Strike while the iron's hot."

"Goody," Ryleigh bubbled sarcastically. She was not going to let Gemma set her up with some egotistical football player. She had enough ego from her ex, Joey, and didn't need to add another problem to the list.

Interest lit Tess's eyes. "If Ryleigh won't go out with him, I will."

Gemma pursed her lips together, shaking her head. "No, Tess. Chas is for Ryleigh," she said decisively.

A thundercloud passed over Tess's face. "Fine," she huffed, crossing her arms over her chest.

"Don't worry, honey, you'll get your turn," Gemma soothed.

The absurdity of the conversation—Tess being disgruntled about a hypothetical relationship—struck Ryleigh as funny. She couldn't stop the peals of laughter from leaving her throat.

Tess and Gemma gave her puzzled looks. "What?" Tess asked.

Ryleigh wagged her finger. "I don't think it's a good idea for the two of you to spend time together. You come up with too many hare-brained schemes."

Tess's hands went to her hips. "What exactly do you mean by that?" she snipped.

Noah tugged at his mom's shirt. "Can we go to the park now?" He sighed in exasperation.

"Yep, you bet." Ryleigh was happy to put an end to this conversation.

Gemma gave her a sharp look. "Don't think this gets you off the hook with Chas."

Ryleigh rolled her eyes.

"I have a sense about these things," Gemma continued. "The two of you would be perfect together. Chas is a good guy, but he'd be even better with the right woman by his side."

"Sure, I'll just run next door and claim the Irish Flash," Ryleigh retorted. She regretted her cattiness when Gemma's face fell. She blew out a long breath. "Sorry, I'm not trying to be mean. I appreciate what you're trying to do, I really do. It's just that I'm not ready for that. I don't need another man in my life," she grumbled under her breath.

"Sure, you don't," Tess harrumphed. "And you don't need air to breathe either, right?"

The comment hit Ryleigh right between the eyes. Before she could say something smart back, Noah clasped her hand with an iron grip. "Let's go," he urged, his eyes bulging like it would kill him to wait another minute.

"All right." Ryleigh shot Tess a look that said, *Go jump in a lake*, but it didn't faze Tess in the slightest. Ryleigh brushed aside her angst at Tess and turned her attention to Gemma. "Thanks for paying my entry fee."

"Of course," Gemma said, smiling.

Tess looked expectantly at her.

Ryleigh let out a loud sigh as her insides softened. It was impossible to stay mad at her little sister. Yes, Tess was annoying as all get out, but she had a heart of gold. "Thank you for signing me up," she pushed through her teeth.

"You're welcome," Tess said in a cheeky tone. She waltzed over to Gemma's side and gave her a tight hug. "All right. I'm off. See ya later."

"Yes," Ryleigh added as she went to Gemma and hugged her. She caught a whiff of Gemma's expensive perfume as Gemma enfolded her in soft, comforting arms. "Thanks for everything," Ryleigh breathed. Gemma was such a blessing. She always ordered twice the amount of food she and Doug could eat in a week. She claimed it was because she liked to have extra in case company stopped by and enjoyed taking food to her neighbors. However, Ryleigh knew Gemma ordered the surplus food to help her out. The extra income was great, but Ryleigh felt guilty about it.

Ryleigh picked up Noah's backpack as she glanced around the kitchen. "Did you get everything?" Last week, they'd left a water bottle and Noah's math workbook. The minute Ryleigh had gotten home, she had to put Noah in the car and come back for those items. She wanted to make sure they got everything this time.

"I forgot my ball," he said, as he ran into the living room. A second later, he returned with it. Gemma walked them out, waving as they went down her walkway to the car. Noah skipped to the car and opened the door. Ryleigh expected him to get in, but he dropped the ball. Before Ryleigh could blink, Noah ran into the street after it. Time seemed to slow to an excruciating pace as Ryleigh saw the approaching car. Tess screamed, but Ryleigh's voice was frozen with terror. Ryleigh heard the squeal of brakes at the same time she caught the flash of movement out of the corner of her eye—a jogger—darted over and pulled Noah out of the path of the car in the nick of time. The force sent them both tumbling to the asphalt.

Ryleigh, Tess, and Gemma rushed to the road as the car door opened. A teenage girl got out, her eyes wide, lower lip trembling. She twisted a finger around a lock of her hair, tears filling her eyes. "H—he just ran out."

Ryleigh's entire body trembled as she went over to Noah and the man. Noah was sobbing, the sound escaping in muffled gulps. Ryleigh helped him to his feet. His knees were scraped and bleeding, otherwise, he seemed okay. Relief swept over her, making her legs go weak. She looked at the man. He, also, had skinned knees and arms. He rose to his feet. "Thank you so much," she said. Tears rushed to her eyes as she hugged Noah. "I thought I'd lost you." She offered a silent prayer of gratitude, trying to calm her heart, which was pounding like a jackhammer against her ribs. Thinking about how close Noah had come to disaster sent shudders slithering down her spine.

She glanced at the man without really seeing him. "I'm so grateful you were there and that you reacted so quickly. Thank you."

He nodded. "You're welcome."

"My knees hurt," Noah whined.

Gemma patted his arm. "It'll be all right." She looked at the teenaged girl. "Everything's okay. No harm was done. You can go."

The girl. Ryleigh had forgotten about her. "Yes," she piped in, flashing an apologetic smile. "I'm really sorry." Thank goodness Noah was fine! Emotion lumped in her throat as she looked at Noah, her hand instinctively going to her heart.

The teenage girl nodded in relief as she hurriedly got in her car and drove away.

"My ball!" Noah stretched out his arms as he looked across the road to where the ball was resting against the curb.

"I'll get it," Tess offered, jogging over to it. A minute later, she handed it to Noah.

"Let's get you cleaned up and bandaged," Gemma said to Noah. Her keen motherly eyes went to the man. "Both of you."

The guy looked down. "I'm all right," he said offhandedly.

"Nonsense, Chas. You're bleeding," Gemma argued. She draped an arm around Noah's shoulders. "We'll see you inside," she said to Chas, in a tone that was more of a command than a request, as she led Noah to the house. Ryleigh jerked as the man's name clicked in her mind. *Chas.* The guy Gemma wanted her to meet.

2

Tess let out a deviant chuckle. "So, you're the Irish Flash," she drawled, giving Chas the once-over. "My, my, you are easy on the eyes."

Ryleigh wanted to strangle her little sister. It was on her tongue to apologize, when she got a good look at the guy. He was a little over six feet tall with broad shoulders and muscular biceps and legs. Her eyes seemed to have a mind of their own as they trailed over the outline of his well-formed chest and flat abs, visible beneath his form-fitting t-shirt. *Sheesh!* Was he real? *Good-looking* couldn't begin to describe this man. He was Superman incarnate with his lithe frame. Well ... Superman with an Irish twist. Ryleigh was unprepared for the heat that blasted her like an oven as her gaze lifted to his. His eyes were a striking blue, the kind of azure blue you could lose yourself in. Her mind took a snapshot of his chiseled features with the faint dusting of freckles over the bridge of his nose. His burnished-copper hair was tapered around the sides, longer and wavy on top. An unruly lock slid down over one eye, giving him a boyish appearance. He swiped it away in a smooth, unconscious gesture.

Ryleigh heard Tess laugh then saw the glint of amusement in Chas's eyes. Her face turned tomato red. Of course, Chas was amused.

She was openly checking him out. Her stomach knotted, and she was ashamed of her lack of restraint. Had she not just told Gemma and Tess in no uncertain terms that she didn't need another man in her life? Now here she was, turning to mush, at the first sight of one. Well, to her credit, Chas wasn't your everyday, run-of-the-mill guy. *Wowser* was the only word that came to mind.

"Hey," he said casually, a grin tugging at the corners of his lips.

"Hey," she repeated dully.

"I'm Chas." He held out his hand. "It's nice to meet you."

Electricity buzzed through Ryleigh as their skin connected. He gave her a firm shake, holding onto her hand a fraction longer than was necessary. Chas tipped his head. "You are?"

"Huh?" Ryleigh asked dubiously, knowing she was coming across as an imbecile, yet she couldn't seem to form a single coherent thought. His voice was deep and melodic, the kind of voice bred from confidence.

Tess laughed in part amusement, part reproof. "He's asking your name."

"Oh. It's Ryleigh," she blurted, eyes widening. *Geez*. Her face was flaming like a beacon.

Recognition lit his features as a slow smile stole over his lips. "You're the one Gemma wanted me to meet."

The ground seemed to shift beneath Ryleigh's feet. "I guess," she mumbled. How embarrassing! Now she'd come across as Gemma's desperate friend who was openly checking him out.

"You're the personal chef, the one who made that fantastic lasagna that Gemma brought over a couple days ago."

Pleasure rippled through her. "Yes."

Chas rewarded her with a smile so brilliant she almost needed sunglasses to filter it.

"My sister's an amazing chef," Tess bragged. "In a month, she's going to be competing in one of the most prestigious cooking competitions in the country."

"Really? That's awesome." Chas seemed genuinely impressed, making him even more attractive. He was a celebrity and yet he was interested in Ryleigh's achievements. "Having tasted your lasagna, I'm sure you'll do great."

"Thank you," Ryleigh murmured.

His eyes held hers. "It's nice to meet you, Ryleigh."

There was something significant in the way he spoke her name, as if he were committing it to memory. His eyes flickered over her with such appreciation that it heightened her senses. Ryleigh became aware of the blood pumping through her veins, the swirling of her cells, how alive and yet befuddled she felt. Luckily, she managed to pull it together before making a complete idiot of herself. "I'm sorry," she began, "I'm a little dazed." She rubbed her forehead. "I'm just so glad you saved Noah. I owe you a great debt of gratitude." Yes, she was a mom, first and foremost. She needed to remember that. She couldn't allow herself to get sidetracked by a good-looking man.

He winked. "I'll be sure and add it to your tab ... for the future."

"The future, huh?" She felt herself smile. "What makes you so sure there will be a future with us?" She was shocked by her own boldness, but now that the words were out, she couldn't call them back. Tess chortled making Ryleigh want to slug her in the gut.

Chas's crystal blue eyes lit with amusement. "Let's just say I have a sense about these things." He gave her a probing look. "Do you want there to be a future?"

For an instant, everything except for Chas disappeared. She was mesmerized, gazing into his arresting eyes. Then, she rocked back, blinking. What had he asked her? Oh, yeah, about the future. She was supposed to answer. "Maybe," she heard herself say as blood rushed to her cheeks. *Sheesh.* She might as well have yelled, *I'm a divorced single mom who hasn't been on a date since the dinosaur age.*

Chas motioned towards the house. "We should probably go inside." He grinned. "You know how Gemma gets if you make her wait too long."

"Yes, siree. Gemma will tan your hides," Tess teased. When the conversation lagged, she sighed. "Well, I'm off. You kiddos have fun." Her eyes radiated innuendo. "Don't do anything I wouldn't," she quipped. "It looks like you got yourself a nice whiff of fresh air, sis," she said, her gaze lingering on Chas. Then, with a wink and smile, she strolled to her car.

Chas tipped his head. "Fresh air. I don't get it."

"Yeah, few people get her," Ryleigh said, trying to mask her mortification.

Chas laughed. "She seems like a character."

"She's something, all right." Ryleigh said darkly, rolling her eyes. A few beats passed, making her keenly aware that it was just the two of them out here.

Chas touched her arm. "Shall we?"

Tingles shot through her. Ryleigh wondered if he felt it too—the sizzling attraction between them. "Yes." Considering her track record with men, Ryleigh probably should've gotten as far away from Chas as she could. She didn't need another complication in her life. When they reached the door, he opened it for her, flashing a smile that melted her insides to ribbons of warm butterscotch. Like the stupid sap she was, she smiled back.

Then again, there was no harm in having a simple conversation with a member of the opposite sex. The world wouldn't stop turning over the event. Maybe she should just take a chill pill and stop analyzing the situation to death. Just because she'd met a charismatic guy, who was easy on the eyes and saved Noah's life, didn't mean she had to fall head over heels for him. She could remain strong and unaffected, right?

Chas was a celebrated Titan's player who could have any girl he wanted. Sure, he'd broken up with his girlfriend, but that didn't mean he didn't have a dozen more girls lined up, waiting in the wings. As they stepped into the kitchen, Chas caught her eye and gave her a lopsided grin that fluttered butterflies in her stomach. All reason flew out the window as she smiled back, surprised by the warmth that flooded her.

It was ridiculous, getting this discombobulated by Chas. She didn't even know his last name. She was making much more of this happenstance meeting than it was. Chas would hang around long enough for Gemma to slap a few bandages on his scrapes, and then that would be that. She could put this silly schoolgirl infatuation aside and focus on the things that mattered. Yes, that's precisely what she'd do. Having resolved it within herself, she felt a little better.

It wasn't until Ryleigh heard Gemma's comment that she knew she was truly in trouble. "Chas, you should stick around for a while." Her eyes sparkled. "Ryleigh has agreed to make everyone dinner."

Ryleigh jerked, but before she could respond, Chas spoke. "Dinner? That sounds great."

There was still Noah's homework to get through, and Ryleigh promised to take him to the park.

"What about the park?" Noah cried, his dark brows darting together in outrage.

Gemma ruffled his hair, her voice ringing with reproof. "Plans changed when you nearly got yourself killed. If you're a good boy, Douglas and I'll take you to get ice cream after dinner ... and we'll go to the toy store at the mall and let you pick something out," she added when the mention of mere ice cream failed to appease Noah.

Noah perked up. "Really?"

Ryleigh wet her lips. "That's very kind of you, but I can't let you do that." She let out a nervous laugh. "Besides, Noah still has homework to do." Also, the last thing poor Doug would want to do when he got home from golfing was babysit Noah for the evening. And for what? So, Ryleigh could be here alone with Chas? The prospect was both terrifying and thrilling.

"I could help Noah with his homework," Chas offered.

For a second, Ryleigh didn't think she'd heard Chas correctly. Was he offering to help with homework? Was the guy actually real or some figment of her imagination?

"I hate homework," Noah grumbled.

Gemma tsked her tongue. "Homework's not that bad. I'll help you with it." She chuckled, tapping her temple with her index finger. "Let's hope there are still enough smarts left in this old brain to count for something." She looked at Ryleigh. "And don't you worry about Douglas and me taking Noah on a little outing. He's like one of my own grandsons." She clasped her hands together. "It's settled." She patted Noah's leg. "All right, kiddo. You're all set. Up you go." She peered over her glasses at Chas. "Your turn."

He held up a hand. "I'm all right. Trust me, I've had much worse on the field."

It was cute and endearing how Chas didn't want to be fussed over. Thankfully, he only had surface injuries. Ryleigh felt bad that he'd gotten hurt helping Noah, yet she was so grateful that he was there. Just thinking about what could've happened to Noah brought mist to her eyes.

"Get over here, tough guy." Gemma waved her arm at Chas. "I won't take *no* for an answer." She squared her jaw, the loose skin under her chin jiggling.

A smile stretched over Ryleigh's lips. "You'd might as well get it over with. Gemma's one stubborn woman."

"That's right," Gemma piped in.

Chas laughed warmly. "All right. Thank you, Gemma, for looking after me. I'll get cleaned up and bandaged, then I'll help Ryleigh fix dinner."

Ryleigh's eyes popped. Help her fix dinner? That would mean working side-by-side, making conversation. Clusters of tingles zinged down her spine.

Chas's gaze settled on Ryleigh, causing her body temperature to spike. "If that's okay with you." There was a question in his bright blue eyes as he awaited her answer.

Ryleigh swallowed, feeling as though she were standing on the edge of a cliff, trying to decide if she should embrace the thrill of living and base jump to the bottom or keep teetering on the edge, looking over. Chas was asking a lot more of her than to simply help make dinner. She got the feeling that once she jumped, there'd be no going back to the way things were before. She caught the encouraging look on Gemma's face. *Let Chas into your life*, she seemed to be saying. The words issued forth of their own accord. "I'd like that."

3

Chas watched in fascination as Ryleigh expertly wielded the kitchen knife chopping veggies for the salad. Her glossy blonde hair bounced lightly on her shoulders with every movement. Surreptitiously, his gaze moved over her slender, petite frame, the defined muscles in her arms rolling underneath the sleeves of her t-shirt. "You're pretty good at that."

"Lots of practice." She offered a quick smile, highlighting her dimples.

Chas wished he could think of something else he could say to earn another of her smiles. "The lettuce is done." Ryleigh had given him the simple task of washing and tearing lettuce for the salad while she worked her magic whipping up a gourmet dinner from scratch. His stomach rumbled at the fragrant smell of parmesan chicken baking in the oven. He rested his back against the counter, folding his arms as he watched Ryleigh lift the cutting board and use the knife to scrape the veggies into the bowl of lettuce. It was interesting how doing something as mundane as cooking could be so thrilling with Ryleigh. "What else can I do to help?"

Ryleigh pursed her lips as she took an assessment. "The chicken needs to cook for another twenty minutes. The pasta is ready." She reached for the wooden spoon beside the cooktop and stirred the sauce before turning the temperature dial down to low. "I think we're good." She wiped her hands on a nearby dishtowel. "The sauce needs to simmer a while so the flavors will meld together." Her eyes widened a fraction as she held up a finger. "Oops, I almost forgot the garlic bread." She pulled a loaf from the refrigerator, along with a stick of butter. "I'll soften the butter in the microwave. Would you mind spreading it on the bread?"

"You bet. So," he began, burning to know more about her, "how did you first get into cooking?"

She removed the bowl of butter from the microwave and tapped it with her finger to check the firmness. Satisfied that it was soft enough, she handed the bowl to Chas and in the process, brushed his hand. He could tell from the way Ryleigh's lashes fluttered that she felt it too. There was a charge of attraction in the room, sizzling the empty space between them. Chas felt the thrill of it, which was akin to rushing down the field full-speed to catch a pass. He was pleasantly surprised to meet such a fascinating woman when he least expected it.

"I've always loved cooking, even when I was very young, I was the one who did most of the cooking for Tess and my dad." She shrugged her delicate shoulders. "I guess it's a part of who I am." The lights overhead picked up the highlights in her hair, turning them to strands of gold. She was stunning, the type of woman whose beauty increased the longer you were around her. She removed the bread wrapper and sliced the bread, placing it on a cookie sheet.

Something she said caught his attention. "So, is it just you, your sister, and your dad?"

A shadow passed over her face. "My mom left when I was ten. I haven't heard from her in several years."

"Oh." He almost said, *I'm sorry*, then thought better of it. He didn't want Ryleigh to think he was pitying her. Chas's large, tight-knit family was such an integral part of his life that he couldn't imagine what it would be like to just have one sibling and an absentee mom. "You and Tess seem close."

"Yes, we are." She bunched her nose. "I mean, she drives me crazy, but she's as loyal as the day is long. She's my assistant."

"That's fantastic." He laughed under his breath. "As much as I love my siblings, I don't know that I could work with any of them."

"How many siblings do you have?"

"Three brothers and one sister." He was amused at how quickly her jaw dropped.

"Wow," she uttered. "Where do you fall in the line?"

"I have one older brother, then there's me, a set of fraternal twins—a boy and girl, and another boy."

"That's a big family."

"Yeah, especially when you consider that my grandmother lived with us when I was growing up. Actually, she still lives with my parents. My grandmother would be very impressed with you."

She tipped her head, her hair falling softly over one shoulder. "Really?" She gave him a quirky smile like she was waiting for the punchline of a joke.

"Yeah, she's always complaining that young girls down know how to cook anymore."

She smiled, her countenance practically glowing. Chas had the feeling of witnessing true inner beauty, the kind that would never dull or grow old. "Did you go to cooking school?"

When she tensed, he got the feeling he'd asked the wrong question.

"I wanted to, but I never got the chance. I enrolled and then found I was expecting Noah." She smiled, a tinge of regret flickering in her eyes. "What is it that John Lennon said? 'Life is what happens to you when you're busy making other plans.'"

"That's so true," he agreed automatically, even though it wasn't true for him. He'd dreamed of playing football for as long as he could remember. His older brother Colin had laughed when Chas told him his dream, saying it was impossible. Colin's merciless teasing had made Chas all the more determined to achieve his goal. Chas's motto had always been, *Tell me I can't do something, and I'll prove you wrong.* He loved the thrill of a challenge. It was what drove him to keep striving to be the best he could be. His thoughts moved to Noah's dad, wondering if he was still in the picture. The thought of Ryleigh with another man sent a pang of jealousy shooting through him. His visceral reaction took him by surprise, especially considering that he and Ryleigh had only just met.

She slid the cookie sheet over to him. He picked up a knife and began liberally spreading butter over the bread. "I hope you're not counting calories," he said glibly.

"Nope." A smile tipped her lips. "You're speaking to a chef, remember? The thicker the better."

"Everything's better with butter, right?"

Her hand went to her lip. "More or less. Do you have to adhere to a strict diet with your line of work?"

"Yep," he said straight-faced. "I do ... a seafood diet."

Interest lit her beautiful face. "Really? Fish is very healthy."

He couldn't contain the smile that stretched over his lips. "I see food and I eat it."

She chuckled, shaking her head.

"In all seriousness, I make a point of eating plenty of fruits and vegetables. Otherwise, I don't have to worry too much about packing on extra pounds." He glanced down at his torso. "Before I got on a regimented workout schedule, I was too skinny."

His blood ran hotter as her eyes flitted over him. "You're perfect now." Her cheeks flushed as she cleared her throat. "I mean, you're the perfect size now."

"Thanks. I knew what you meant." A strong connection buzzed between them as he winked. He slathered on more butter. "Tell me about Noah's dad," he prompted casually. He held his breath, awaiting her answer. Maybe it was too soon to pry, but he wanted to know her situation before he got too wrapped up in her. He grunted inwardly. Who was he kidding? Ryleigh already had him intrigued. She'd gotten to him when he caught the look of tenderness in her eyes as she hugged Noah, right after realizing he was okay. Ryleigh had depth and feeling—something his previous female companions had been sorely lacking. She was down-to-earth and real. Also, she didn't seem to be caught up in the fact that he was a football player.

"His name is Joey. He and I have been divorced for four years."

"I'm sorry," he replied, elation sweeping over him.

She sighed. "It happens." She paused. "The good news is that Joey and I are friends."

"How old was Noah when the divorce took place?"

"Three."

He processed this bit of information. "So, he probably doesn't even remember the two of you ever being together."

"No."

"Noah seems like a good kid." The task of buttering the bread now done, he placed the knife in the sink.

"Yes, he is." Her eyes softened to a warm gold as a smile tugged at her lips. "He's an endless ball of energy." She shook her head. "I still can't believe he ran out in the road." Her expression grew tortured. "If you hadn't been there today…" Her voice trailed off.

Without thinking, he stepped closer and placed a hand over hers. "But I was there." He had the urge to pull her into his arms and discover the taste of her perfectly formed, red lips. Instead, his free hand went up to caress her hair. Her breath caught as desire flickered in her eyes. The sparks between them were incredible. Was this really happening? Something changed in an instant as the flame died in her eyes. It was replaced with a wooden guardedness. A second later, she withdrew her hand and stepped back.

"I'm sorry," she said, offering a consolation smile. "You seem like a great guy … but I can't do this."

Her rejection stung. "Is there someone else?" Just because Ryleigh was divorced didn't mean there wasn't a guy in her life.

"No, there's no one else."

That was the best news he'd heard all day. He wanted to punch a fist in the air and shout, *Hallelujah!* Then again, she was giving him the brush-off, so all was not well. "So, it's the old *it's not you but me routine*," he joked lightly. "I get it. You're just not into me. It's okay."

Color blotched up her neck. "No," she sputtered, "it's not that at all. Believe me, if it were just up to me, I'd jump on you in a heartbeat." Her eyes flew open wide. "Um, I didn't mean for it to come out that way."

He laughed. She was adorable when she got embarrassed. He was relieved to know that he hadn't misread the signals.

"It's just that ... I have to think about Noah and what's good for him," she continued, a note of remorse in her voice.

His lips turned down as he tried to understand her reasoning. "Do you think I'd be bad for Noah?" What had he done to give her that impression? He loved kids ... wanted a houseful of them one day.

The words spilled out of her mouth. "No, not you personally. I'm just saying that I can't afford to make another mistake." Her mouth drew into a tight line. "I'm sorry."

"Who says I'd be a mistake?" Even as he asked the question, he couldn't help but think that this conversation was premature. *Geez.* He'd not even asked her out. All he did was place a hand over hers to comfort her. Well, that's not all. The intent to kiss her had been there.

He wanted to kiss her right now! He wanted it badly.

She turned her attention to the stove, leaving Chas to wonder how the situation had taken such a wrong turn. The wise thing to do would be to just move on. There were plenty of women who'd jump at the chance to go out with him. But those women weren't Ryleigh. Somehow, in a way he didn't understand, he knew she was different from the rest. He studied her erect posture, her shimmering sheet of hair that bounced like sunlight off water with her every movement. His eyes moved to her slim waist and curved hips. He wanted to get to know her, wanted to find out what made her tick. It surprised him how much he wanted those things.

In the time it took her to turn back around, a plan began to take shape—a way to ensure that he could spend time with Ryleigh. "How about a friend?" he asked casually. "Do you have room in your life for that?"

Time seemed to stand still as she mulled over his question. Finally, she tipped her head, a relieved smile overtaking her features. "Yes, that would be nice."

Great! Now he was one of those pathetic dweebs relegated to the friend zone. At least it kept his foot in the door, gave him a chance to get to know her. Part one of the plan was initiated.

Noah bounded into the room. "Homework's done," he announced.

"Fantastic," Ryleigh boomed.

Chas made a fist and held it out to Noah who bumped it with his fist. "Way to go, bud," he drawled.

"Yeah!" Noah responded exuberantly as he flashed a large smile, causing dimples to form. Noah had Ryleigh's smile, but his features and hair were dark.

Gemma came in. "Something smells good. What did you make?"

"Parmesan chicken," Ryleigh answered with a hum in her voice. "When's Doug getting home?"

"I just talked to him. He's on his way." Gemma glanced at the clock on the microwave. "He should be here in about twenty minutes."

Ryleigh nodded. "Perfect."

Chas looked down at his shorts and t-shirt. He was just beginning his jog when he saved Noah, so he wasn't sweaty. Still, he'd like to put on some other clothes. "I may run home and change right quick …. If that's okay with y'all."

"Sure," Gemma said with Ryleigh nodding in agreement.

Gemma caught Chas's eye. He could tell that she was burning to know how things were progressing between him and Ryleigh. When Gemma mentioned that she wanted to fix Ryleigh up with Chas, he assumed that Ryleigh wanted that too. Obviously, that wasn't the case. Interesting that Gemma thought the two of them would be good together, despite Ryleigh's standoffishness.

A curious light settled in Gemma's eyes. "Noah, did you know that Chas is a football player?"

Noah's lively eyes sparked with interest. "Really?"

"Yep, sure am," Chas answered.

"When we go to the toy store tonight, we should look for a football," Gemma suggested. "I'm sure Chas wouldn't mind teaching you how to throw it."

Chas would teach a hundred kids how to throw a football if it gave him an opportunity to see Ryleigh again.

Noah's brows creased. "I already know how to throw a football," he countered indignantly, shooting Chas a hard look.

A laugh rumbled in Chas's throat. He glanced at Ryleigh, the corners of her lips quivered like she was trying not to laugh. Their eyes met as they shared a moment. Chas turned back to Noah. "All right, sport. We'll just toss the football back and forth. No instruction. How's that?"

"That'd be okay," Noah said nonchalantly with a shrug.

"What do you say?" Ryleigh prompted, reproof sounding in her voice.

"Thank you," Noah replied dutifully like he was reading a script.

"You're welcome," Chas answered.

Ryleigh brought her hands together. "Dinner's almost ready." She motioned with her head. "Go wash your hands."

Noah's shoulders dropped a mile, along with his face. "Do I have to?" he whined.

She gave him a firm look. "Yes, you do."

"Fine," he huffed.

"I'm sorry," Ryleigh said to Chas as Noah left the room.

Gemma shook her head, her eyes radiating amusement. "Well, look at the bright side. He'll keep you humble."

"Yes, he will," Chas said. *Him and his mama, both*, he added mentally. It was refreshing to know that he was being weighed and measured by his own accord, not because of his profession. Anticipation streaked through Chas as he thought about the upcoming evening. They'd eat the delicious dinner that Ryleigh prepared and then Gemma and Doug would take Noah on an outing, meaning Chas could have some alone time with Ryleigh.

He tried to figure out why he was so taken with a woman he'd only just met. Sure, Ryleigh was beautiful, but he was used to being around beautiful women. Selena his former girlfriend was a knockout. When he first saw Selena at a party, hosted by one of his fellow Titan players, he'd been taken by her extraordinary beauty. However, the more time he spent with Selena, the more he came to realize that while she was gorgeous on the outside, she was an empty shell within. She was consumed with fashion, shopping, and climbing the social ladder. As time passed, Chas began to suspect that Selena's interest in him was due to his notoriety and money, not because of the man he was inside. Their relationship was going nowhere, which is why Chas broke up with her.

Chas was ready for a relationship of substance with someone he could relate to. Was Ryleigh that woman? His pulse picked up at the thought. Ryleigh had a natural elegance and warmth that drew him in, making him want to discover the mystery behind her striking hazel eyes, fringed with thick, dark lashes.

Chas marveled at how he happened to be there precisely at the right time to save Noah. He grinned inwardly thinking how his grandmother would say it was owed to the luck of the Irish. Chas almost didn't go jogging today. Selena had been calling and texting, asking him to accompany her to a charity dinner. He decided last minute that he was for sure not going. It was better to draw a clear line so that Selena would realize the two of them were over.

Now, here he was, trying to figure out a way to get Ryleigh to give him a chance. It was astounding the difference a few short hours could make in a person's life. Ryleigh was determined to keep him at arm's length, but one way or another, he had to persuade her to go out with him. She was the kind of woman who could get under a man's skin, make him yearn for the impossible. Then again, Chas's MO was taking the impossible and making it possible.

It worked for football. Could he make it work for a relationship? He took in a deep breath. Only time would tell.

"I'll be back in a jiffy," he said, rushing out so he could get back around the same time Doug got home.

4

After dinner, Chas helped Ryleigh clean up the kitchen while Gemma and Doug took Noah on the promised outing. Ryleigh could see the tiredness behind Doug's eyes, could tell he wasn't keen on the idea of going back out shortly after he got home, but he was a good sport about it. Doug adored Gemma and usually gave her whatever she wanted. "We'll take our time," Gemma chirped as they left. "The two of you should go for a walk. It's nice outside. There's a full moon," she added, her voice going juicy.

Chas looked at Ryleigh for a reaction.

"Sure, I'd like that," she said casually, even though the thoughts of being alone with Chas kept slamming her heart against her ribcage like a boxer against the ropes. Add a romantic full moon and it revved the intensity up even more. Ryleigh was trying hard to come across as cool on the outside while her insides were roasting at five hundred degrees.

Gemma was right. The moon sat plump and full in the center of the sky. The delicate orange and yellow blend reminded Ryleigh of Colby Jack cheese. The evening held enough moisture to give the air a chill, making Ryleigh glad she'd worn her jacket. She'd almost left it at home this morning, but grabbed it as an afterthought. If someone had told her this morning all that would transpire today, Ryleigh wouldn't have believed it. It still boggled her mind to think that she was getting the chance to participate in the Grilling and Chilling Cooking Competition. That, in and of itself, was a huge blessing. Then, she met Chas. Simply being in his presence made everything more brilliant. The food they'd eaten tasted better, the night air smelled clean and fresh, and the gentle breeze kissed her skin, making her feel exquisitely alive. The historic neighborhood with the stately homes and large trees was magnificent anyway, but tonight Ryleigh got the feeling they were walking in some magical place where feet had never tread before.

"Which direction?" Chas asked.

"It's your neighborhood. You tell me."

His mouth formed a decisive line, emphasizing his strong, angular jaw. "All right. I'll take you on part of my jogging route. Since it's evening, we can cut through the golf course." He pointed. "This way, madam." He bowed slightly, making a flourish with his hand.

A giggle bubbled in her throat. "Thank you, kind sir." She set off with a light foot, feeling as though she were floating.

"I want to hear more about you," Chas said when they'd gone a few paces.

She gave him a sidelong glance, struck by how incredibly handsome he was. The moonlight gave the illusion of his rugged features being carved from stone like a Greek statue, infused with strength and confidence, not of this world. If only she could borrow a hundredth of his confidence, maybe she could rid herself of the incessant whispers that slithered around her, driving home the point that she'd never be good enough to truly succeed. She shook off the negative reminder of her inadequacy. "What do you want to know?"

"Let's see," he mused, "where to start?"

She laughed dryly. "My life's not that exciting, trust me."

"To you maybe because it's old hat, but I find everything about you fascinating."

Heat simmered through her as she caught the meaning of his words. "That's laying it on thick, considering you hardly know me."

He laughed easily. "Does it scare you that I find you fascinating?"

Yes! her mind screamed. *It terrifies me.* Her mouth formulated a single word in response. "Why?"

She sensed his surprise. Then amidst the glow of the moonlight, she saw a wry grin slide over his lips. "Well, for starters, you don't seem to realize how wonderful you are. I find that refreshing."

She felt herself smile. "You probably say that to all the girls."

"No, I don't."

His matter-of-fact answer took her off guard. *Sheesh.* She didn't know how in the heck she was going to manage being just friends with Chas when she was so drawn to him. That's the way it had to be for Noah's sake though. Never would she put her own wants and desires over Noah's. She wouldn't make the same mistake her parents had.

"Did you grow up in the Dallas/Ft. Worth area?"

"Yes, in the Crowley area of Ft. Worth. How about you? Where are you from?" She wasn't about to let him ask all the questions. Ryleigh wanted to find out more about Chas too.

"New Orleans."

"Ah, I thought I detected a slight accent."

He turned to face her, his brows furrowing with mock offense. "Hey now," he drawled, "I sound Southern, the same as you."

She held up a finger. "Yes, you do, but when you said dinner, you didn't pronounce the 'r'. It sounded more like dinnuh. Your words are more lyrical, sprawling. I like it," she assured him. "It sounds classy with the French twist."

"Thank you," he said heartily.

"What's it like in New Orleans? Are you a jazz lover?"

"You betcha."

"Who are your favorites?"

He thought for a moment. "Louis Armstrong, Fats Domino, Harry Connick, Jr."

She tipped her head. "Is Harry Connick, Jr. from New Orleans?"

"Sure is."

"Makes sense. He kind of sounds like you. Do you go to Mardi Gras?"

"I did a few times when I was in high school, but not now. Things get a little crazy."

She grunted. A pro football player who looked like Chas would be fresh meat for all the women. "I can only imagine." A few beats passed, the silence stretching comfortably between them, as if giving them adequate space to express themselves. "What's your family like?"

He chuckled. "I thought I was asking the questions."

"Not hardly," she countered. "Hold your horses, Irish, you'll get your turn."

His rich laughter warmed the space between them. Ryleigh marveled at how larger-than-life Chas was. His very presence made her tingle all over. Chas was the type of guy who commanded attention wherever he went. Why he seemed taken with her was a mystery. When he spoke, her mind jumped back to attention. That's right, he was answering the question she'd asking him earlier.

"My family's big, loud, and rowdy, but we love each other."

The affection in Chas's tone evoked a sense of loss. When Ryleigh was a kid, she'd wished for a big family ... or at least a complete family with two parents who were engaged and caring rather than being consumed with their own wants and desires. "Are any of your brothers football players like you?"

"They played in high school, but nope, I'm the only knucklehead in the family who made a career out it," he joked. "My oldest brother Colin works in finance. My dad keeps hoping he'll join the family business, but so far it hasn't happened."

Her interest was piqued. Ryleigh loved hearing entrepreneurship stories. "What type of business?"

"My dad started out with a string of sporting goods stores. Now he has a conglomerate—several restaurants, rug cleaning companies, and equipment rental stores."

Her throat tightened as she swallowed. "Oh, wow. That's impressive." Ryleigh assumed Chas made a bundle of money playing for the

Titans, but from the sound of this he'd grown up wealthy. Chas and her were from two different worlds, further proof that there could never be anything more than friendship between them. Chas had never wanted for anything, whereas Ryleigh had been fighting her whole life to get ahead.

"Something's bothering you. What is it?"

She flinched, surprised that he'd picked up on her internal turmoil. She forced a laugh. "Nothing. I'm fine."

"Liar," he shot back.

She whirled around, eyeing him. "What did you call me?" She was part amused, part irritated.

A lopsided grin tugged at one corner of his lip. "You heard me. I can tell something's going on in that pretty head of yours."

Pretty. The compliment sent a golden glow over her as she rolled it around in her head a couple of times. She got a few steps ahead before realizing that he'd stopped in his tracks. Just as she turned to look back, he tugged on her hand, sending fireworks sparking through her.

"What's wrong?" he persisted. Still holding her hand, he pulled her closer. Her blood did a wild swirl as she looked up at him and saw the longing on his face. Her eyes seemed to have a mind of their own as they moved over his rugged features, drinking him in. "I love your freckles," she mused, almost to herself. She noticed a faint scar, a couple inches long, running from his right eye to his cheekbone. Instinctively, she touched it. "Football?"

"No, a BMX bike when I was eleven."

She laughed. "What happened?"

"Colin my older brother and I dragged storage boxes out of the garage and set up a ramp. We jumped the boxes, adding an extra one each time." He wrinkled his nose. "Colin jumped seven. I said I could jump eight. I almost made it too, but my front tire fell short of the ramp, and I took a nosedive."

She winced. "Ouch."

"Yep, I was a bloody mess." His eyes sparked with amusement. "I don't know which was worse—the injuries or my grandmother's tongue lashing."

A smile curved her lips. "I'll bet you were a cutie when you were young—the all-American kid with red hair and blue eyes."

"I was gangly and awkward." He rumbled out a self-deprecating chuckle. "I can't count the number of fights this ugly mop got me into when kids called me carrot head. My parents were just thankful when I grew old enough to play football, so I could channel my energy into something productive."

She touched his hair. "I love it. It suits you. I'm guessing no one calls you carrot head now."

"Not to my face, anyway." His jaw hardened a fraction with determination.

She continued walking, getting several steps away from him. She glanced back over her shoulder, flashing a coquettish smile. "You coming?"

"I'd rather just watch you," he murmured.

The look in his eyes caused desire to simmer in her stomach. Everything in her wanted to run back to his side, throw her arms around his neck, and kiss him until the need for him subsided. Where in the heck were these thoughts coming from? She was supposed to be disciplined, controlled. Her tongue was telling Chas that she wasn't ready for a relationship, yet her heart had other ideas. Here she was, flirting with him. She was pathetic! Still, she couldn't seem to help herself. A devilish thought circled in her head. Did she dare do it? "All right, carrot head," she quipped, "let's go." She quickened her step to a near jog.

"I see how it is," he drawled behind her.

For a split second, she wondered if he'd just let her keep on jogging. No sooner had the thought entered her head than he closed the distance between them and lunged for her, grabbing her waist. The force sent her spiraling forward. She squealed, fearing she'd fall, but he caught her, holding her tight.

"Hey, no fair," she protested amidst peals of laughter. He maneuvered her around to face him, keeping a tight hold on her waist.

His intense blue eyes moved over her face as if he were absorbing every detail. "Now what're you gonna do?" he taunted in a low, husky voice that hummed a craving for him through her chest. With a swift movement, he pulled her close. Anticipation did a mad swirl down Ryleigh's spine, her blood thrashing like restless waves against her temples. Keeping one hand firmly fixed on her waist, Chas's other hand went to her hair as his finger traced the length of one of her tresses. Heat from his body seeped into hers, wrapping her in invisible warmth.

"Call me carrot head again," he taunted, a faint amusement glittering in his eyes. His hand moved to her jaw. With tantalizing feather lightness, he trailed the tip of his finger over her skin. The sensation was thrilling, sensuous, making her want to throw caution to the wind and jump off the edge into the wonderful unknown, losing herself in the feel of Chas's lips.

"Carrot head," she whispered, eyes meeting his in a challenge.

The instant the words left her tongue, his mouth came down on hers, tender and coaxing at first, then more urgent. A tidal wave of pleasure rushed through her as her hands slid around his neck. He dipped her, arching her back as he deepened the kiss, causing her heart to skyrocket to the moon above. His lips lit a flame that seared a path from her mouth to her toes, her body quivering in response. When he pulled back, ending the kiss, her mouth was still burning with fire. She rested the flats of her palms against his hard, muscular chest, trying to catch her breath.

"Wow," he uttered, a large grin overtaking his features. "You're amazing."

She blinked a couple times, trying to get her bearings. "You're amazing too," she admitted. *So much for the friendship thing.* She searched herself, trying to discern her feelings. Getting involved with a football star wasn't a good idea, yet she didn't feel a ton of remorse about it. The kiss had been extraordinary—the best! Still, there was Noah to consider. "Chas," she began, "I don't think this is a good idea. I have a young son and a business to take—" She stopped mid-sentence when he put a finger to her lips.

"I know." He gave her a sheepish grin that made him look boyishly adorable. "I stepped out of line. It won't happen again."

The disappointment that sat like a brick in her stomach took her off guard. "It won't?"

He winked. "At least not tonight."

She laughed, despite herself, shoving his arm. "You're impossible."

"That's what they tell me," he responded easily. He stepped away from her and motioned with his head. "Come on. I wanna show you the golf course. It'll look incredible in the moonlight."

As they walked side-by-side, he reached for her hand and linked his fingers through hers. She should've protested, but it felt so good to have her hand in his. Being here with Chas was amazing, exhilarating. That was the problem. How was she supposed to go back to normal life after this? "I don't even know your last name." She winced, thinking how irresponsible it was to kiss a guy without at least getting that tidbit of information.

"O'Brien."

His hand was warm, his grip firm but not too hard. "Ah, makes since. It's Irish. Which one of your parents is Irish? Or is it both?"

"My dad and grandmother. My grandmother immigrated with her family to the US when she was a teenager." A sentimental laugh rumbled in his throat. "Although you'd never know my grandmother grew up in the US. She has a thick Irish brogue and flaming red hair."

"Redder than yours?"

He laughed. "Oh, yeah. Mine's nothing compared to hers. And, she has a temper to match it."

"She sounds like Tess … without the red hair, of course."

He paused, thinking it over. "I can see that."

When they reached the golf course, Ryleigh's eyes widened as she took in the rolling hills and valleys, covered in a plush carpet of deep-green grass. The landscape was kissed in the soft glow of the full moon overhead. Ryleigh had the urge to run full speed onto the course and dance wildly like a kid. "This is beautiful," she breathed. She turned to Chas, realizing that he was studying her.

"Yes, you are," he said.

She flashed an appreciative smile. "Mr. Charming."

He squeezed her hand. "Just speaking the truth. If that gives me brownie points, then so be it."

She wasn't sure how to answer. Thankfully, he didn't seem to be expecting her to say anything. He led her along the sidewalk, which looked silver in the muted light. Ryleigh was burning to know more about him. "What's it like to play professional football?"

He tipped his head like he was carefully considering her question. "It's an adrenaline rush to be out on the field with the stadium packed with fans, knowing that the next play will either be my salvation or my condemnation."

She made a face. "That sounds stressful." She was keenly aware of the feel of her hand in his.

"Oh, it is, but I love it. It's what I've always wanted to do. On the off season, right now, I work out every day—mostly my own regimen. I meet with a personal coach/trainer once a week to go over fundamentals, so I can remain sharp in my skills."

"Have you played for the Titans long? Sorry," she added, "I don't follow football."

He let out a low chuckle. "Nor I cooking."

Her lips quivered with the need to smile. "I guess we're even."

"Last season was my first with the Titans. I played for the Georgia Patriots before that."

"How do you like Texas?"

A sly grin slid over his lips. "It's great right now."

Her cheeks warmed, realizing he was referring to her.

"Texas has its good and bad. The summers are brutal, but the winters are great. I mean, there are few places in the US where you can go for a walk in January, wearing only a sweatshirt and jacket."

"True."

"I'm sure you've heard the saying … 'Never ask a guy if he's from Texas …'"

Ryleigh picked right up, adding in the next part. "'If he is, he'll tell you.'"

"'If he's not, you'll just embarrass him,'" they both finished.

"Texans are patriotic, which I like. They're proud to be Texans and proud to be Americans, in that order."

"Amen," Ryleigh quipped with gusto, mirth rippling through her. "Have you been to the stockyards?"

"Yep, but only once."

"Did you go to the rodeo?"

"No, I haven't done that yet."

"What? You've gotta do that. It's such a huge part of the culture here."

"Maybe I will ..." his eyes swung towards hers "...if you'll take me."

She took in a quick breath, an unexpected blanket of warmth covering her. "I can do that," she finally said.

All too soon, they arrived back at Gemma's house. Chas was still holding her hand. As subtly as she could, Ryleigh extricated her hand from his.

His eyes lit with amusement. "Good idea. We don't want to get Gemma all excited, thinking she succeeded in fixing the two of us up."

The irony in his voice wasn't lost on her, but she sidestepped the innuendo. "So, that's your house." She motioned to the large, stately brick home next-door.

"Yep," he said, stating the obvious. "It's a bit of a drive from here to the Titan's Sports Complex, but I wanted to live in a neighborhood that reminds me of home."

"I love historical homes."

He smiled broadly. "Something we have in common. Stick around, and I might even get you hooked on football."

She was coming dangerously close to being hooked on a certain football player.

"When can I see you again?" he asked, searching her face.

She blinked rapidly. "I'm not sure. I come to Gemma and Doug's house once a week. I'll be here next Tuesday."

"A week?" He shook his head, his lips forming a tight, agonizing line. "It's no good. I can't wait that long to see you again. How about dinner tomorrow night?"

Her heart leapt. "Dinner?"

"Yeah, you know, the thing where we sit down at a table across from each other, and they bring us food."

She gave in to the smile tugging at her lips. "That sounds suspiciously like a date."

"Oh, no. We're just friends." There was a playful mocking edge to his voice. He reached in his pocket and pulled out a phone. "What's your number?"

The moment of truth was here. Was she going to continue forward with Chas or call it quits?

"Come on," he urged, "take a chance. It's just one dinner."

"Tomorrow night's a school night," she hesitated. "Noah usually has lots of homework."

"I can come over early and help, and then we can take him with us," he offered in a practical tone like the dilemma was solved.

"No!" She regretted her outburst when she saw the confused look on Chas's good-looking face. She searched for a way to explain her reasoning as delicately as possible. "I want to keep Noah out of this, so things won't get complicated."

His jaw twitched. "Meaning until you're sure that I'm up to snuff."

"Huh?" She'd never heard the phrase *up to snuff* before.

"That I'll make the cut. You don't want Noah developing a relationship with me if you're not sure where this is going."

"Yes," she admitted. "Sorry. Noah has to be my top priority."

"Of course. You'll get no argument from me, there. This is not a competition. I just want to be part of your life."

His words seeped into her thirsty heart, as if he'd discerned her innermost desires. She wanted to find someone—a companion with whom she could share her life. She'd thought she found that before, but how dreadfully wrong she'd been. Lots of guys seemed great at first glance. It was when you got to the fine print that the problems began.

His beautiful eyes searched hers. "So, what's it to be, Ryleigh—"

He pushed out a low chuckle. "Now I'm the one at a loss. I don't know your last name."

She lifted her chin, feeling vindicated for her reservations. "See? This thing is moving way too fast."

"I don't think fast is necessarily a bad thing," he uttered, his voice a caress.

"You would say that, Irish Flash," she grunted.

His expression reflected appreciation and surprise. "I thought you didn't follow football."

"I don't. Gemma told me your nickname," she explained.

"Ah, Gemma's been talking me up. I'll have to thank her later." Ryleigh looked at his strong, firm lips, remembering how they'd felt against hers. He seemed to be reading her thoughts as he smiled. "Just give me your number, Ryleigh …"

"Eisenhart's my last name."

His lips parted as he drew back. "That's an awesome name. Eyes and heart. The minute I saw you with my eyes, you captured my heart," he mused.

Ryleigh expected him to laugh and say he was kidding, but he didn't. He just kept staring at her with those piercing eyes that had the power to see into her soul. He stepped closer, his voice controlled and persuasive like he was negotiating. "Give me your phone number. I'll text you, and you can let me know tomorrow if you can go to dinner. How's that?" Time stood still as she tried to decide what to do. "Tell me, Chas O'Brien, has there ever been a time when you didn't get something you wanted?"

An intimate smile stole over his lips. "Well, I guess that remains to be seen. Please," he urged, his eyes darkening with an intensity that evoked a powerful longing in her chest. When she stammered out her phone number, a triumphant smile overtook his features. "Thank you."

"Aren't you going to put it into your phone?" She realized with a jolt that she wanted to make sure he had her number. Why was she being so wishy washy? One minute telling herself that she only wanted to be friends with Chas. The next, kissing him like there was no tomorrow.

He tapped his temple. "I've got it."

The lights in Gemma's living room popped on. "They're back. I'd better go."

She turned to leave, but he caught her hand and gazed into her eyes. "Ryleigh Eisenhart?"

Her heart skipped a beat. "Yes?"

He lifted her hand to his lips where he planted a kiss. It would be a while before her skin lost the memory of his cool, soft lips. "It was a pleasure meeting you. I'll see you tomorrow ... for dinner," he added meaningfully, leaving her no *out*. The second he released her hand, she gave him a quick nod as she hurried into the house, fighting the temptation to look back.

5

Ryleigh was in her home office with Tess beside her, each of them sitting behind their desks. "Thanks. We'll see you after while," Tess said, as she put down her phone with a frustrated sigh. "That was Molly Satterfield. She asked if she could switch her appointment today from ten to eleven thirty. She's worried her garden club meeting will run over. I told her that would be fine, but it'll push us to get everything done in time before you have to pick up Noah. I already made the ingredient list for her dishes. We'll need to run by the store and pick up some items beforehand."

"Sounds good," Ryleigh said absently, not taking her eyes off the computer screen.

"Tomorrow will be tricky. We have the Stevens at nine, and then we're going to the Magleby's at one. I can run out and grab Noah from school. I hope that Cathy Magleby won't mind having Noah there while we finish up."

"Uh, huh." Ryleigh surfed through the images of Chas on the web. Some were of him clad in football uniforms during games. Others were of him dressed in tuxes and suits at charity events. Her gaze took in his handsome features, the determined set of his chin, his muscular build. He reminded her of an Irish Superman. Tingles circled down her spine, thinking of how wonderful it was to be with Chas, almost like a dream. That was an appropriate description, a beautiful dream. Unfortunately, dreams faded into memories the moment you woke up.

This morning, her fears had resurfaced with a vengeance. She couldn't afford to make another mistake. Her heart clutched when she saw several pictures of the same woman on Chas's arm—a tall, willowy, dark-eyed beauty with long, lustrous hair. Was this the ex-girlfriend that Chas had recently broken up with? Ryleigh glanced at the article to learn the woman's name, Selena Simpson. She typed in the name along with Chas's. It brought up several society page articles. Yes, the two of them had been a couple. Selena was a successful model and fashion consultant with her own line of jewelry. Hot prickles covered Ryleigh before she went stone cold. She and Selena looked nothing alike, nor did they have any similarities in interests. Ryleigh felt like the country cousin compared to this glamorous, ritzy woman.

Tess rolled her chair over. "You haven't heard a single word I've said. What're you so interested in?

"Nothing." Ryleigh tried to click out of the article, but it was too late.

"Ah, I see." A sly grin curved Tess's mouth. "I take it your date with Chas went well."

"It wasn't a date," Ryleigh countered, her cheeks going flush. "We're just friends."

"Sure, you are." Tess laughed. "You don't need a man, right?" She shoved Ryleigh's arm.

"Cut it out," Ryleigh grumbled.

Tess gave her a perceptive look. "You like him ... a lot." She pointed to the computer screen. "Pull up that image you were just looking at." Her brow creased. "Who's that woman draped over Chas's arm?"

Tess had always been able to pick up on Ryleigh's frustrations and worries. "It's nothing," Ryleigh said casually, "just a charity event. The woman was Chas's date."

A wicked grin spread over Tess's lips. "I think you finally found your man."

"No," Ryleigh spurted. "We're just friends."

Tess rolled her eyes. "Yeah, you keep saying that. 'The lady doth protest too much, me thinks,'" she chirped. "When're you gonna see him again?"

Ryleigh wet her lips. "Well, he asked me to go to dinner with him tonight." She wouldn't even have told Tess, but Ryleigh had about decided to go, and she would need Tess to watch Noah.

"That's awesome!" Tess hooted.

"Would you mind watching Noah?"

"Absolutely."

Ryleigh trailed her hand through her hair, trying to express the thoughts tumbling like an express load of laundry in her brain. "I don't know if going to dinner with a celebrity's a good idea."

"Why not?"

"I dunno. What if it doesn't work out? Do I really want to put myself and Noah in the limelight?"

"What if it does work out? Have you even thought about that?"

Ryleigh grunted. "Considering my track record, what would be the odds?"

"Just because you've made a couple mistakes, doesn't mean that you're doomed for life, sis. Give it a chance. Chas seems like a great guy."

"Yeah, they all do at first."

Tess made a face. "I could've told you that Joey was trouble from the get-go. I did try to warn you, as a matter of fact."

"I know." Ryleigh rolled her eyes. "Must we go into that again? I should've listened to you. Are you satisfied?"

"Only if you'll listen to me now." Tess's eyes were pleading as she touched Ryleigh's arm. "Give Chas a chance. You deserve some happiness, sis."

Ryleigh folded her arms over her chest, drumming her fingers. "It's just dinner, after all."

A broad smile split Tess's face. "Exactly. Have you looked up how much he makes?"

"No." Her forehead wrinkled. "I wouldn't be going out with him because of his money."

"Still." Tess pumped her eyebrows. "I'll look it up." With a burst of energy, she rolled back to her computer and began clattering on the keyboard. A second later, her eyes bugged. "Wow."

"What?" Ryleigh asked, curiosity getting the better of her, as she wheeled her chair over to Tess.

"According to Wikipedia, Chas used to play for the Georgia Patriots."

"Yes, that's what he told me."

"While Chas was with the Patriots, an injury sidelined the starting running back, opening a window for Chas to step in. After leading the Patriots to a series of wins, Chas signed a four-year deal with the Titans last year for a hefty $25 million-dollar contract."

Ryleigh's throat went drier than the Mohave Desert as she swallowed. Her first thought was relief that Chas was sticking around for another three years. The second thought ... that kind of money was inconceivable. She and Chas really did live in two different worlds. It was foolish to think that the two of them could date. "Maybe going to dinner with him is a bad idea."

"Shh, listen," Tess prompted, turning her attention back to the screen. "This is Chas's second year with the Titans. Last season, your boy rushed over 1,100 yards, had five touch downs and 378 yards receiving." Her eyes glittered with a star-struck quality. "Your new boyfriend's a superstar."

"Whose new boyfriend?" Joey asked, as he strolled into the room and plopped down on the nearby loveseat, crossing his jean legs in a wide stance with his ankle resting on his thigh.

Crap! The last thing Ryleigh needed was Tess blabbing about her romantic life to her ex-husband. Ryleigh and Joey were in a good place now, but that didn't mean Ryleigh wanted to flaunt her boyfriend in front of him. She cringed. Yes, she'd just thought of Chas as her boyfriend. Ryleigh zoned in on Tess, mentally begging her sister to put a sock in it. Even though Tess knew exactly what Ryleigh was getting at, she pointblank ignored her.

"Ryleigh's dating Chas O'Brien, the Titan's football player." She said it smugly, taking great delight in rubbing Joey's nose in it. Even though Ryleigh met Joey through Tess—he was her best friend Natalie's brother—the two of them didn't get along. Tess thought Joey was a loser who shirked responsibility. That was true on some levels. After all, part of the reason why it didn't work out between them was Joey being a big kid who couldn't hold down a steady job or handle the responsibility of a wife and child. The last straw was when Ryleigh had gone to the grocery store and left Joey to look after two-year-old Noah. When Ryleigh returned home, Joey was so caught up in playing a video game that he wasn't even aware Noah was no longer in the house. Noah had wandered several houses down.

Ryleigh tried hard to give Joey the benefit of the doubt. While the two of them would never again share anything romantic, Ryleigh considered Joey a friend—to the point where he could come and go as he pleased in her home, evidenced by how he strolled in just now without knocking.

A stunned look came over Joey as he tipped his head. "How's that?"

"Ryleigh's dating Chas O'Brien," Tess repeated slowly like Joey was mentally challenged. Her eyes glittered with satisfaction when Joey's suave face drained, giving his olive tone skin a sallow look. "My sister's found herself a good guy." She flashed a cherubic smile at Ryleigh. "I'm so excited about how everything's working out."

Ryleigh shot Tess a look that could kill, but Tess just laughed it off, fiddling with her hair.

Joey's dark eyes sought Ryleigh's. "Is that true?"

"We're mostly friends," Ryleigh answered. *Mostly friends?* Why in the heck did she say that?

A deviant chuckle trilled out of Tess's throat. "Yeah, I'll take a friend like that any day. Chas signed a $25 million-dollar contract with the Titan's last year. Plus, he's easy on the eyes, if ya know what I'm saying," she drawled, in an exaggerated southern accent.

Joey forced a smile, his eyes remaining on Ryleigh. "You and O'Brien. That's cool." He began playing with his Converse shoelace. "How did the two of you meet?"

"He lives next door to one of Ryleigh's clients," Tess supplied.

Joey pursed his lips, nodding. "Rad." He tapped on his shoe.

Ryleigh could tell that Joey was unnerved by the news, but he was trying to put on a good face. Thin and wiry, Joey was handsome with dark eyes, thick lashes, and spiky, dark hair. Noah looked so much like him. His witty sense of humor had drawn Ryleigh in. She'd had such high hopes for the two of them and the future they'd build together. Instead, she had to step up to the plate and become the breadwinner, so she could give Noah a good life.

"What're you doing here at nine in the morning? Shouldn't you be at work?" Tess asked, her voice laced with accusation.

Joey looked down at his shoelace. "Things didn't work out at Net Leads." He lifted his head, anger flashing in his eyes. "My boss is a dufus. I'm taking a couple weeks hiatus before I start applying for more jobs."

"Sounds about right," Tess smirked.

Joey was a computer coder. His skills were in such high demand that he had no problem getting hired, but he did have a problem keeping a job.

"So, tell me more about this thing you've got going with Chas O'Brien." Joey's voice was conversational, but Ryleigh caught the edge in his tone. Also, the faint lines around his eyes tightened.

Ryleigh wanted to pummel Tess. She shot her sister a dark look, trying to figure out a way to diffuse the situation.

"He's taking Ryleigh to dinner tonight," Tess supplied.

Joey's eyebrow shot up. "Really?" He stroked his chin, looking thoughtful. "You sure you wanna go down that road?"

"Why wouldn't she?" Tess asked.

Ryleigh's stomach tensed. "What do you mean?"

Joey spread his hands, a benign smile ruffling his lips. "I'm all about you dating and having fun, but you can't afford to have another Dylan Ellis situation."

An invisible fist dug into Ryleigh's gut.

Tess's voice rose. "Seriously? You're bringing that up?"

Joey held up a hand. "Down girl. I'm just playing the devil's advocate. A guy like Chas O'Brien's probably out with a different girl every night. I just don't want Ryleigh to get her hopes up, start thinking this is more than it is." He looked at Ryleigh. "You know I'm right."

Ryleigh swallowed. A year ago, Ryleigh let Tess talk her into going through an online dating service. She met Dylan Ellis. He was handsome, had a great career as a dentist, was funny, attentive. Long story short. Ryleigh fell hard. She allowed him into her life. Noah got attached to him. She thought she'd found the one until she found out he was married.

"Think about it for a minute," Joey continued, "you and Chas O'Brien live in different universes. Not trying to be mean, but he can have any girl he wants. Why would he be interested in you?"

A cold sweat broke out over Ryleigh. She clutched her fists to keep her hands from shaking.

"Because Ryleigh's beautiful and accomplished," Tess countered. "Of course he'd want to go out with her."

"Yes, you are those things, Ry," Joey said, his voice going soft. "No one's prouder of you than me. I'm just trying to keep you from making a big mistake. You've got to see this for what it is. You'll be just another notch on Chas O'Brien's belt."

"You're such a jerk," Tess spat. She turned to Ryleigh. "Don't listen to him. He's just trying to undermine you. Chas is a good guy. This is not another Dylan Ellis situation," she said vehemently, giving Joey a blistering look.

A humorless smile spread over Joey's lips as his eyes cut into Ryleigh's. "For your sake and Noah's, I sincerely hope that's the case."

Tess tipped her head sideways, a new light coming into her eyes. "Joey, you look a little puny. Have you been sick?"

"I'm fine," he said tersely.

"Really? You don't look fine." She leaned forward. "You've got dark circles under your eyes like someone punched you."

Ryleigh took a closer look. Tess was right. Joey's skin had a sickly pallor, and his cheeks looked hollow.

"Maybe you should go home and get some sleep instead of sticking your nose where it doesn't belong," Tess said.

His brows darted together. "Ryleigh is my business."

Tess barked out a laugh. "No, she was your business until you blew it. You and my sister are old news. The sooner you get that through your thick head, the better."

6

Chas was finishing up the last set of his lower body free weight workout in his home gym when he got Ryleigh's text.

Sorry, but I won't be able to make it tonight.

His insides knotted as he plopped down heavily on the bench, draping his towel over his shoulder.

How about tomorrow night instead?

He clutched his phone, waiting for her response. A couple minutes later, she texted back.

This isn't going to work.

Disappointment rattled through him. Last night, everything had gone so well. Sure, Ryleigh kept insisting that they could only be friends, but her lips said otherwise. *That kiss.* It had lodged inside him, making him long to see her again. She was real, down-to-earth.

He'd sprint a thousand yards to have her gaze at him again with her soulful hazel eyes, ringed in gold.

He swiped the beads of sweat pooling on his forehead, trying to figure out what to do. Maybe he shouldn't do anything. Ryleigh obviously wasn't interested in dating him. Selena sent him four texts, today alone, saying she missed him and wanted to get together to talk.

An image of Ryleigh with her soft, blonde hair and wispy smile flashed through his mind. He had to see her again. He balled his fist. Ryleigh was different from the cookie cutter girls he'd dated, a breath of fresh air. The thoughts of going out with Selena again after meeting Ryleigh didn't sit well in his gut. Ryleigh got under his skin in a way no other girl had. All morning long, he'd carried around his phone waiting for her text, praying that she would agree to go out with him. He blew out a long breath. Determination made him the man he was. He didn't back down from a challenge. Ryleigh was afraid. That's why she was running in the other direction. She said she couldn't afford to make another mistake, meaning she'd had bad experiences in her past—most likely with her ex, maybe more. Chas would do what it took to earn her trust. A woman like her was worth working a lifetime to win. Her goodness reminded him of his grandmother and mom, the two women he most adored. He wanted to find someone loyal whom he connected with. He wanted a long, abiding relationship like his parents had, and he wasn't about to find that with Selena or any of the other Titan groupies.

He really didn't know why he felt such a strong push to find the right one now. He jerked as a sudden thought occurred to him. Maybe it was because he had found the right one. His dad always talked about the importance of timing and how he'd known with every fiber of his being that Chas's mother was the right one when he met her. "We Irish have this innate sense that makes us more perceptive to these types of things. We recognize our other half." Chas had heard that his whole life. For much of his life, he'd just chuckled thinking his dad was a sentimental sap. Now, however, he didn't find it a laughing matter. The urgency to pursue Ryleigh was so tangible he could almost taste it.

Time to put part two of the plan into place. He dialed a familiar number.

"Gemma, hello. It's me, Chas." He rubbed his forehead. "Hey, I'm wondering if you could help me out with something ..."

As Ryleigh pulled into Gemma's driveway, the strings of her heart pulled taut as her gaze went to Chas's house. It had been a week since she met Chas and spent the magical evening with him. After her text where she told him it wasn't going to work, he'd not responded back. She was surprised at how disappointed she was that he didn't continue to push her. Then again, why would he? She'd shot him down in no uncertain terms. Clearly, he'd gotten the message and moved on. Too bad she couldn't do the same. Too bad she was still thinking about him, brooding over the fact that she'd missed her chance.

It was better off this way, although Tess didn't agree. She was furious with Ryleigh for not keeping the date with Chas. She accused Ryleigh of being a coward and a sell-out. The sisters had gotten into a huge argument over it, and the tension was still lingering between them. Ryleigh got out of her car and opened the back door to grab a grocery bag loaded to the brim with food and cooking gadgets. Her pulse kicked up several notches as she tried to figure out what she'd say if she saw Chas.

Disappointment sat heavy on her chest when she reached Gemma's door. No sign of Chas. She punched the doorbell a couple of times before Gemma answered. Her face lit with a smile when she saw Ryleigh. "Hello," she said cheerily. She looked past Ryleigh. "Where's Tess?"

"She stopped at the grocery store to pick up a few items that we were missing." She held up the bag. "These are the things I had on hand at my house."

"Oh, sounds good. Come on in."

Ryleigh placed the heavy grocery bag on the island, flexing her arms to relieve her strained biceps. She reached in the bag and pulled out her apron. She was about to tie it around her waist when Gemma stopped her. "Um." She moistened her lips. "I hope you don't mind, but there's been a slight change of plans." Gemma looked nervous.

"Is everything okay?" Ryleigh's first thought was that Gemma or Doug might've gotten a concerning medical report. Chills raced through her. She didn't want anything bad to happen to either of them. There were like family.

A strained smile stretched over Gemma's lips. "Yes ..." she hesitated.

Ryleigh leaned forward, wanting to pull out whatever it was Gemma was trying to say.

"I don't want you to prepare meals for me this week."

Ryleigh's heart dropped as a thousand thoughts bombarded her. "Is everything okay with you and Doug?"

"Oh, yes," Gemma laughed, "we're great."

"Are you okay financially?" It was probably the entry fee. Gemma had spent all of her disposable income on that and didn't have any left to pay for the meal prep.

"We sure are."

Ryleigh's throat thickened as she swallowed. "Is it me? Something I've done?" she squeaked.

Gemma put a reassuring hand on her arm. "Oh, no, honey, you're great." She fidgeted with her hands, shifting on her feet.

An impatient laugh escaped Ryleigh's mouth. "Just spit it out, Gemma."

"It's about Chas," she blurted, looking relieved to have gotten it out.

The air left Ryleigh's lungs. "What?"

Gemma flashed an apologetic smile. "I'm sorry to do this to you, but Chas needs your help this week more than I do."

Ryleigh's heart began to pound. "I don't understand. Help with what?"

"His meals."

"That's absurd," Ryleigh snapped.

"I told him that I'd let him have my slot. He's willing to pay you twice your usual fee."

The hair on Ryleigh's neck stood on ends as blood rushed to her head. "He had no right to contact you and interfere with my business," she fumed.

"I know, you're right," Gemma said in a placating tone, "but he really needs your help."

"Sure he does," Ryleigh retorted.

Gemma gave her a pleading look. "Please, it would mean a lot to me if you'd go over and work for him today."

"But what about you and Doug? You need meals."

"I know." Her face brightened. "You know what. I have an idea. Tess can make them for us. I'll pay for her, just as if you were here. Then, you'll be making triple the pay."

Ryleigh felt like she was spinning out of control, like a fan that had no *off* switch. "Is Tess behind this?" Anger coursed through her veins.

"No, no," Gemma said, talking fast. "She knows nothing about it. I thought I'd call her right now and ask her to pick up double items—enough for me and Douglas ... and Chas."

An incredulous laugh rippled in Ryleigh's throat. "I can't believe Chas put you up to this," she grumbled. As irritated as she was at Gemma, she was madder at Chas. At the same time, she was strangely flattered and excited to see Chas again. Her hand went to her hip. "So, I'm just supposed to waltz over to Chas's house and prepare his meals? Just like that?"

Gemma offered a large smile. "Yes."

She shook her head. "Gemma, I know you mean well, but all this isn't necessary ... first, the contest entry fee and now this. I'm a big girl and can take care of myself."

"Of course you can," Gemma soothed. She gave Ryleigh an encouraging look. "Now, go on over to Chas's house and do your thing."

"My thing," she repeated dully.

A hesitant laugh left Gemma's lips. Her movements were jerky like she was flustered. "You know what I mean. I'll call Tess and tell her to pick up double."

"She'll need to grab the things I have in the grocery bag too."

"Oh, yeah. Let me get a pad and pen, and I'll jot those things down."

When the list was complete, Ryleigh had no choice but to pick up the grocery bag and go next door to Chas's house. She was fuming, ready to bite Chas's head off. To think, a few moments ago, she'd regretted giving him the brushoff. It seemed like she'd made the right decision. She didn't appreciate being manipulated, especially concerning her livelihood. Gemma meant well, but her interference wasn't helping matters. Balancing the grocery bag in one arm, she jabbed the doorbell with a finger. A few seconds later, Chas answered.

"Hey," he said with such a jubilant expression in his electric-blue eyes that all the anger left her in an instant. "I'm so glad you're here. You look fantastic." He reached for the grocery bag. "Here, let me."

"Thanks," she uttered, his compliment finding a place in the tender spot of her heart. What was it about Chas that caused her to feel myriad emotions all at once?

"Come on in."

She closed the door behind her and stepped into the tall foyer that opened to a large living room. The furnishings were modern and streamlined with a variety of grays, browns, and blacks. Very masculine. She followed him into the large combination family room and kitchen, her eyes tracing the outline of his wide shoulders and tapered waist. His every movement was fluid, his steps as light and nimble as a panther. A burst of attraction shot through her, sending heat rushing to her face. Could she handle spending the next few hours alone with Chas? Without flinging her arms around him and kissing him again? It was easier to think with her head when she was away from him. Now that she was here ... not so much. She was back to square one.

Chas deposited the bag on the island. He rested his back against the counter as he folded his arms over his chest, giving her a bird's-eye view of his cut biceps. His long legs were encased in faded jeans, and his blue t-shirt picked up the color in his eyes, making them look so strikingly blue it looked like he was wearing tinted contacts. His gaze scoped over her with such appreciation that she almost wondered if he were really looking at her. "How've ya been?"

So consumed with you that I haven't been able to focus on anything else was the first thought that rattled through her head. "Good. Busy with work."

"How's the preparation going for the cooking competition?"

She was impressed that he remembered. "Fairly well. I've been making a few dishes, going through the trial and error phase."

He nodded, his brow creasing slightly like he was mulling something over. "I thought that might be the case." A lopsided grin tugged at one corner of his lips. "So, were you surprised when Gemma sent you over here?"

Her eyes narrowed as she met his gaze full on. "That's one way to put it."

"You were ticked."

"Pretty much."

"I know, I'm sorry. It was a lousy thing to do. I just couldn't think of any other way to see you again." The longing in his eyes evoked the same feelings within her, making her think she'd gotten Chas O'Brien all wrong. After learning the depth of his stardom and listening to Joey, she'd convinced herself that she was only a passing fancy to Chas and that it would be better to nip things in the bud before she got hurt. However, standing here in front of him, all the feelings and impressions she had when they first met were resurfacing. Her heart began to pound. There were some things she needed to know right up front. "Why was it so important for you to see me again? What is this thing between us, to you?"

He laughed, the smooth tone of his baritone voice flowing over her like a ballad. "You don't beat around the bush, do you?" He sounded impressed.

"No, I can't afford to, not with Noah."

An electrical surge shot through her veins when he stepped closer and gathered her hands in his. "I want to get to know you. See where this thing could lead. Is that so bad?"

The tenderness in his expression made her come dangerously close to breaking down all her defenses.

"I don't know what's happened to you in the past, but I can fill in the blanks. You've been hurt."

"Yes." She felt small and vulnerable. She swallowed, determined to keep the moisture in her eyes at bay.

"I will always be up front and honest with you."

The sincerity in his voice was convincing. "Why me?" she squeaked, clearing the frog in her throat.

He looked puzzled. "I don't understand."

A humorless laugh rumbled in her throat. "What is it about me that you find appealing?"

An unencumbered smile filled his face. "Well, for starters, you're beautiful and down-to-earth."

She rolled her eyes. "Yes, I am that...down-to-earth," Was that a good thing? Down-to-earth seemed mundane and boring. Had the glamorous model broken up with Chas? Was he on the rebound?

"I love your tentative smile and the depth of feeling in your expressive eyes. You're like a mystery that unfolds a little at a time."

She laughed, wrinkling her nose. "That's a little over-the-top."

His eyes lightened as he released her hands. "Okay, I've told you some of the things I find attractive about you. Now it's your turn."

She coughed. "Excuse me?"

"Time to fess up." He lifted his arm and flexed his muscle, causing his bicep to bulge like a grapefruit. "It's these guns, right?" he teased.

Her spirits lifted. "Yes, most definitely. I was thinking of going out with Popeye, but when I saw those..." she tsked her tongue "...I decided on you instead."

He laughed, giving her an appraising look. "You're good," he drawled. A couple of beats stretched between them. "Seriously. I wanna know what you like about me." His eyes flickered with determination. "I'll keep hounding you until you tell me."

"You know, I believe you would."

"Absolutely," he shot back.

"All right," she relented with a chuckle. "You're easy on the eyes, as Tess put it." Her cheeks flamed when the words left her mouth. "You make me laugh."

"Yes, I seem to have that effect on people. The quintessential entertainer." He made a goofy face and shuffled his feet. "Dance monkey, dance, right?"

She shoved his arm. "No, I didn't mean it that way. It was a compliment."

"Thank you," he said genuinely, appreciation glowing on his face. "What else?" he asked eagerly.

"You're fun to be around. You keep me guessing." Her eyes went to his lips, a wicked thought playing in her head. "You're not a bad kisser."

"Hey," he groaned. "Not bad? I'll show you a kiss." A hint of a quirky grin stole over his lips as he roughly pulled her into his arms. "Let me lay a big one on you, darling," he said in Texas cowboy drawl.

She averted her face, laughter bubbling in her chest. "Ew!"

He held her close, planting wet, sloppy kisses on her cheek and neck as he made smacking sounds.

"Yuck!" she protested.

A moment later, he pulled back, assessing her with an innocent expression. "What's wrong? You don't find me attractive?" Laughter flashed in his crystal eyes.

She rested her palms against his chest, fighting the urge to run her hands over the definition of his muscles.

"I can unequivocally say with zero hesitation that I didn't find that one bit attractive."

The moment slowed as his eyes deepened with intensity. "How about this?" he asked, his voice going husky. Lightly, he kissed a corner of her mouth, sending tingles rippling down her spine. His lips moved to the other corner. "Or this?" he murmured.

She felt like a teenager in a tailspin over her first crush as she breathed in his masculine scent, intoxicated by his nearness. Her lips parted instinctively as his mouth crushed hers. His lips were demanding, exploring as his hands moved to her back. A tiny groan escaped her lips as she melted into him, surprised by her own eager response. Her hands went to his neck as she clung to him. It wasn't just the heady desire swirling around her like a tornado that got to her, but the tender ache in her chest that whispered of a connection stronger than she could've imagined. She discovered the feeling of home in a place she least expected it—Chas O'Brien's arms.

He pulled back, his hand cupping her cheek in a tender embrace, a sense of wonder in his eyes. "This doesn't come along every day," he uttered with a certainty that settled truth into her bones. He gave her a pleading look. "Tell me it's not just me that's feeling this way."

"No, it's not," she admitted softly.

He rewarded her with a dazzling smile, his eyes drinking her in. "You wanna know what it is about you that I find so irresistible?"

"Yes."

"When you mentioned all the things you like about me, there was nothing about football or the Titans. It was all me."

She caught his vulnerability, appreciated him opening up to her. She'd not given it any thought before, but she realized with a start, that it would be hard to be a celebrity and never know if someone loved you for you.

He chuckled. "You didn't even know my last name."

"I know." Her eyes widened. "I only found out after we kissed." She winced. "I still can't believe I kissed you the first day we met."

"I thought I kissed you."

She laughed, feeling as buoyant as a balloon. "So, Chas O'Brien, where do we go from here?"

He pursed his lips. "Well, for starters, I'm hoping you can whip us up some lunch. Then, we'll go have some fun."

"Hah! I can't do that. I've got to make your meals for the week. Plus, Noah gets out of school at two-thirty."

"How about dinner then?"

She rocked back. "Tonight?"

"Yeah, if you can." He rubbed his hand up her spine, evoking shivers of delight. Ryleigh wondered if she'd ever stop feeling so in awe of Chas.

She chewed on her lower lip. "I'd like to, but with it being a school night ..."

"Friday then. Come on. It'll be fun," he urged.

"All right." Tess usually had a date on Fridays, so Ryleigh would have to find someone to watch Noah. Gemma, maybe. After all, it was the least Gemma could do considering how hard she'd worked to fix her up with Chas.

A large smile stretched over Chas's lips. "Awesome." His eyes lit with a peculiar light. "So, what did you think about the kiss?"

"Hmm ..." she mused, "I'm not sure."

His face fell. "What? You're killing me here, smalls," he joked.

She did feel small and petite in his strong arms. She liked it. "I think I need another kiss," her eyes went to his lips, "just to be sure."

"I'm happy to accommodate," he uttered, as his lips took hers in a long, pulse-pounding kiss. Ryleigh lost herself in the feel of him, her spirit soaring.

"Uh, he—llo."

Ryleigh jerked, pulling away from Chas like he was a hot coal. "Tess, what're you doing here?" Blood rushed to her cheeks.

"I rang the doorbell, but I can see you were otherwise occupied." Tess flashed a shrewd grin.

Ryleigh frowned. "That was fast. I figured it would take a while to pick up all the extra ingredients."

"I was in the car, headed to Gemma's house when she called. I figured it would be easier to drop off the items at Gemma's and then come over here to take an assessment of everything you need." Her eyes danced with mischief. "Although from the looks of things, you're not getting much cooking done." She laughed. "Let me rephrase that. You're cooking, just not the kind of cooking I thought."

Ryleigh cast a dark look at Tess. She looked at Chas to get his reaction. He was amused. Ryleigh relaxed, letting a grin overtake her face. "All right. You got us."

"Anyway, we should probably talk about the menu for Chas." She flipped the ends of her hair.

"She's supposed to be my assistant," Ryleigh said to Chas, "but sometimes I wonder who's working for whom."

"Just keeping things moving along," Tess answered breezily.

"We should talk about the types of foods you like. Whenever I start working for someone, I interview them, find out their dietary needs. That way I can tailor the meals to your specific needs."

"I'm easy," Chas said with a flick of his hand.

"Easy on the eyes," Tess added under her breath.

Ryleigh wanted to shrink to the size of a bug and crawl away. Her sister could be so annoying. A look passed between Chas and Ryleigh. She knew he was thinking how she'd used Tess's words earlier.

"What did I miss?" Tess asked, looking back and forth between them.

"I was just telling Chas that you shouldn't keep throwing around compliments, giving him a big head."

"Ah, is that what's happening here?" Chas asked. "It's all right, Tess. I appreciate the compliments. You build me up and your sister keeps chomping me down to size. It helps balance things out."

"Hey," Ryleigh protested.

"I knew I liked him," Tess said decisively. An impish grin curled her lips. "So, did you finally convince Ryleigh to go on a date?" she asked Chas.

"Yep, sure did. This Friday."

Tess's features tightened with concern. "Shoot, I've got a date this Friday. I won't be able to watch Noah." Her head ducked slightly into her shoulders. "Sorry."

Ryleigh pursed her lips. "No worries. I'll see if Gemma can watch him."

Tess shook her head. "That won't work either. Gemma just told me that she and Doug are going to Houston this weekend to visit their daughter and grandkids."

"We can take Noah with us," Chas offered.

Ryleigh's stomach knotted. Her apprehension must've shown on her face because Chas touched her arm. "It's okay." She didn't know what he meant by that. Was he saying it was okay for him to get to know Noah? Or was he saying it was okay that she was hesitant for him to become part of Noah's life? She forced a smile. "I'll find someone to watch him."

"Get Joey to do it," Tess said. "He doesn't have a lot going on right now. I'm sure he'll be glad to watch him. It's the least he can do, since Noah's his son," she added tartly.

A funky tension settled into the room. Ryleigh could tell that Chas was uncomfortable with the conversation. "Yeah, I'll work it out," Ryleigh said evasively, cutting her eyes at Tess. If only her little sister could learn to keep her mouth shut, things would be so much easier.

Tess put her hands together, getting down to business. "All right. What do you want me to pick up?"

"We can go and grab the items," Chas inserted.

Ryleigh tipped her head. "Really?"

"Sure. Maybe you could get some of the items that you need to make the test food for the competition. You could try out those dishes on me." He grinned. "I'll be your guinea pig."

"That would save me some time," Tess said. "I could get all of Gemma and Doug's meals made and even pick up Noah from school. That way, you'll have plenty of time to do—" she twirled her hand "— whatever." Her eyes radiated amusement.

"Are you sure you don't mind picking Noah up?" Ryleigh asked.

"Not at all. You can just come home afterwards. I'll hold down the fort, help Noah with his homework, feed him dinner, put him to bed. No need to rush home," Tess chirped.

Chas touched Ryleigh's arm, the warmth and pressure of his strong fingertips seeping into her flesh. "I like the sound of that. I get you all to myself."

"Yep, it's a date," Tess said, a goofy grin spilling over her lips. A peculiar look came over her face as she looked at Ryleigh before turning her attention to Chas. "Despite what my sister says, she needs a good guy like you in her life." She squared her chin, her eyes flashing. "Don't break her heart."

"Tess!" Ryleigh exploded, heat combusting over her.

Chas turned, locking eyes with Ryleigh as he spoke, conviction ringing in his voice. "Don't worry, Tess. I have no intention of fumbling the ball. When fate throws you the pass of a lifetime, you hold onto it with all your might and run it straight to the end zone. End of story."

7

There was a certain feeling that Chas always got before taking the field—the unleashed energy of lightning building before an electrical storm, the heightening of the senses, the surety of being invincible and knowing that victory is yours for the taking. The adrenaline that surged through him during these times was like an intoxicating wine that he could never drink enough of. That's exactly how he felt right now with Ryleigh. They were in the produce section of the grocery store, selecting ingredients for the dishes Ryleigh wanted to make him, and he felt like he was king of the universe with her at his side.

She picked up a cantaloupe with her slender fingers and brought it to her nose, inhaling deeply, her soft, blonde tresses falling forward in the movement.

He made a face. "What're you doing?"

"Selecting a ripe cantaloupe."

"Aren't you supposed to tap it or something?"

Amusement curved her features. "No, you smell it at the stem. If it has a strong scent, you know it's ripe."

He quirked an eyebrow. "Really?"

"Really. Try it." She held the cantaloupe out to him. When he sniffed it, she shoved it into his face.

"Hey," he protested, but she just laughed. After selecting a cantaloupe, she moved to the vegetables. It was fascinating to watch how discriminating she was as she selected the perfect ones. "This is an art for you," he observed.

A smile tipped her lips. "Yes, I suppose it is."

"What's for lunch?"

She pursed her lips. "How does teriyaki salmon, wild rice, seared asparagus and mango salsa sound?"

Chas's mouth watered. "All that for lunch?"

"Yep," she hummed, giving him a radiant smile that flowed warmth through him like the sun illuminating a dark corner of a room.

His fingers trailed lightly over the naked skin on her arm as he gave her a lingering look. He leaned close and whispered in her ear. "Can we have dessert first?" He took great delight in the cute apple-polish flush that rose in her cheeks.

"Don't push your luck," she said with a straight face, but her eyes were soft with amusement.

"Well, hello," a cheery voice said.

Chas turned, his heart plummeting to the floor when he saw who was approaching. "Selena." He fixed on a polite smile.

"Darling," Selena purred, "you've been a hard man to find." She stepped up to give him a kiss on the lips, but he averted his face last minute so her lips grazed his cheek instead.

"What're you doing here?" he demanded, glancing at Ryleigh whose face had gone rigid.

"I went to your house." Her botoxed lips formed a petulant pout. "You weren't there, of course. I was headed home, happened to glance at the grocery store parking lot, and saw your Mustang." Her hand went up to toss her mahogany hair, and then she caught hold of her purse strap. Chas could tell from the tight way she squeezed it that Selena was nervous. She knew she was intruding. Her gaze darted to

Ryleigh as a large, fake smile spread over her lips. "Hello. I don't believe we've met." She thrust out her hand. "I'm Selena Simpson."

"Ryleigh Eisenhart." The two women shook hands.

An awkward silence passed. Instinctively, Chas stepped closer to Ryleigh. He wondered what she was thinking right now. As always, Selena was dressed to the nines. However, she looked over-processed and plastic, the bulk of her beauty owed to a salon or medical spa. Ryleigh, however, was the real deal. Seeing the two women side-by-side made Chas more certain than ever that he preferred Ryleigh. The knowledge surprised him with how new his relationship was with Ryleigh. Still, that's how it was. He felt a burst of relief and exhilaration, like he was finally on the right path. He'd gotten the same feeling when he started playing pro ball, experiencing the culmination of all his hopes and desires.

Selena gave him an accusatory look. "Are the two of you together?"

He glanced at Ryleigh, saw her hesitation. It only took him a second to decide how to respond. "Yes," Chas answered emphatically as he slid his arm around Ryleigh's tense shoulders. He locked eyes with Ryleigh silently pleading with her to agree with him, not just to let Selena know he was off the market. More importantly, he wanted Ryleigh to reciprocate his affection. He squeezed gently. "Isn't that right?"

"Yes," Ryleigh finally answered softly, her cheeks reddening.

Anger flashed in Selena's eyes, her lips forming a tight line. "That was quick. How did the two of you meet?"

"Ryleigh's my ..." He tried to figure out how to answer.

"His personal chef," Ryleigh inserted.

Selena barked out a derisive laugh. "That's convenient."

"I think so," Chas said. He turned to Ryleigh. "It works nicely. She does the cooking, and I do all the cleanup," he joked.

For an instant, Ryleigh's eyes widened in surprise. Then, a tiny smile played on her lips. "That's good to know."

Selena's cool eyes raked over Ryleigh with such open malice that it sent a shudder slithering down Chas's spine. Then, just like that,

Selena's expression changed to one of interest as she tipped her head. "You know, I've been thinking of hiring a personal chef. Do you have a card?"

No! was Chas's first thought. He didn't know what evil plan was spinning in Selena's head, but whatever it was couldn't be good.

Uncertainty clouded Ryleigh's eyes, turning them a dark green.

"You don't have to give her your card," he said, looking back at Selena who reminded him of a coiled cobra, about to strike. How could he have ever found her attractive? She was a pretty poison.

"So, you're giving your little girlfriend instructions?" Selena mused. She grunted a laugh. "That figures. I guess you found someone you can control, huh?" she taunted.

The comment was a slap in the face. "You know what, Selena," Chas countered. "I hoped we could end things amicably. I guess that's not the case."

Selena shot Ryleigh a nasty look. "Good luck, honey. Enjoy your minute in the limelight ... until Chas finds your replacement." She lifted her nose in the air with a sniff and turned on her heel, flouncing away, her stilettos clicking like rapid gunfire against the hard floor.

"I'm sorry about that," Chas began.

Ryleigh's eyebrow arched. "I take it that was your ex?"

"Yeah." He rubbed a hand across his forehead. "A big mistake," he muttered with a self-deprecating laugh. Then, he got a good look at Ryleigh, his stomach tightening when he saw her wooden expression. "Don't let Selena get to you. She's just mad because I broke up with her."

Something indiscernible flashed in Ryleigh's eyes.

"What?" he asked, his heart lurching. Things had been going so well and Selena had to ruin it!

"How long were you and Selena together?"

He wondered where this was going. "I dunno." He thought back. "Six months, maybe. Why?"

The next words cut through Ryleigh's mouth like razor-sharp

arrows "I just wondered how long I have before you'll trade me in for a newer model."

A disbelieving laugh rose in his throat. "What?"

Ryleigh's eyes were gold and green swirled marbles, her jaw set in stone.

His mouth went dry as he swallowed. "Where is this coming from?"

She barked out a laugh. "After that woman's display, it should be obvious what I'm getting at." She spoke the word *woman's* like it was a curse word, her eyes flashing.

"Selena was just saying those things to get under your skin."

"Well, it worked," she fired back. She took in a breath. "You know what? I knew this was a bad idea."

He tensed. "How can you say that?"

"I told you, I don't have the luxury of being wrong about you." Her voice quivered with intensity.

"This is ludicrous! Are you really going to just take everything Selena said at face value? She's a jealous wench."

"One that you obviously thought well enough of to date." He tried to answer, but she held up a hand to stop him. "If that's the kind of woman you're used to—" she exhaled a bitter laugh "—then you have no business doing whatever this is with me."

His mind whirled. "Yeah, I was attracted to Selena. She's a beautiful woman." The words died on his lips when he saw Ryleigh's stricken expression. Then her face turned several shades darker, her lips vanishing in a defiant line. Fearing Ryleigh might flee, he caught hold of her arm. "Let me finish. All right?"

"Fine," she muttered through clenched teeth.

"When I got to know Selena, I realized she was a hollow shell, which is why I broke up with her. I told myself then that I wanted a woman of substance. A woman who was as beautiful on the inside as she is on the outside."

Ryleigh's eyes grew moist. "And you think I'm that person?"

"Yes." He paused, gazing into her eyes. "I know you are." For a second, he thought he was getting through to her, but then a shadow crossed her features.

"You say that now, but how will you feel six months from now?"

He'd been on the goal line before, now he was getting pushed back by a string of penalties. He studied her face. "I don't know how I'll feel," he said, needing to give her an honest answer. "But I'm willing to take a chance to find out." He tried to make sense of the conflicting emotions battling in her eyes. "What is it that you're so afraid of?" He touched her hair. "Don't be afraid to let me into your life."

She stepped back, a guarded expression on her face. "Let's just get our shopping done, okay?" Her voice had a high-pitched, unnatural edge.

"Okay," he finally relented as she turned her back to him and reached for the grocery cart, quickly pushing it away from where he stood. He watched for a minute, then numbly followed her.

CHAS WAS RIGHT. Ryleigh shouldn't have let Selena get to her. The woman was a spoiled, rich diva. The problem was that Selena had exposed Ryleigh's greatest fear—the one that repeatedly screamed that she'd never be good enough. Ryleigh knew she struggled with self-confidence. Viewing images of Selena Simpson online, draped over Chas's arm at various social events was bad enough. However, seeing her in person was a thousand times worse. Selena was so glamorous and put together that she hardly looked human. How was Ryleigh supposed to compete with a woman like that?

Sure, Chas said that he wanted Ryleigh because she was beautiful on the inside too. However, even he couldn't predict what would happen in the future. Was she brave enough to open her heart again? The breakup with Joey had been brutal. Then, Ryleigh picked up the pieces and put her life back together. She took a chance on Dylan Ellis and opened herself up again. When she found out that Dylan was married, she was not only heartbroken but humiliated. She swore she'd never get herself into a compromising situation again. Chas was a bright, shiny star that lit up the sky, making everyone take notice. He was from a different world than her, lived by a completely different set of rules. Ryleigh got the feeling that if Chas broke her heart, she'd never fully recover.

There were times when Ryleigh wished she could be more like Tess, living in the moment without worrying incessantly about the future. However, Ryleigh had Noah to think about, whereas Tess was footloose and fancy free. Maybe Chas would be true to her. Maybe they'd have one of those storybook romances that Ryleigh had only dreamed about. Even in a best-case scenario, Ryleigh's entire life would change if she got serious with Chas. She and Noah would be thrust into the spotlight. She wasn't ready for that, and it wouldn't be fair to subject Noah to unnecessary stress. Noah had latched onto Dylan, getting closer to him than he was to his own dad. The distraught look on Noah's face when he realized Dylan would no longer be part of their lives still haunted Ryleigh. Noah had cried for a week. Ryleigh couldn't—wouldn't put her son through that again. She glanced at Chas's rugged profile. He sensed her gaze and looked at her.

"Are you okay?" he asked in concern. They were in the car, headed back to Chas's house.

"I'm fine," Ryleigh answered curtly. No, she wasn't fine. She was a wreck. She was weak. Regardless of how many of these little talks she had with herself, she kept ending up in Chas's arms. Even now, her cells cried out for him. She sat up straight in her seat. She had to be strong and resist. Getting involved with Chas could only spell trouble. Ryleigh couldn't go there right now. Maybe when Noah was older, but not now.

When he reached for her hand, a flame leapt through her. As delicately as she could, she removed her hand from his. "I'm sorry," she mumbled as she turned to stare out the window, her mind getting lost in the blur of the passing houses and buildings.

8

Ryleigh was here in body, but there was a wall between them. Her movements were jerky and mechanical as she worked to prepare lunch. Chas wanted to go to her side, pull her into his arms, and smooth away the stress lines from her beautiful face. He should probably find another way to occupy his time rather than standing over her, but something in him wouldn't rest until he'd made her smile. He pulled out a barstool and sat down, propping his elbows on the counter. He could tell from Ryleigh's rigid jaw and narrowed eyes that he was making her uncomfortable.

Ryleigh was about to chop an onion for the mango salsa. She cast him an accusing look. "Are you just gonna sit there and watch me all day?" she grumbled.

"Yes," he answered matter-of-factly with a light laugh. "Unless you'd like some help."

She paused, considering his offer. "Sure, you can chop the onion."

He wrinkled his nose. "Really?" He hated chopping onions because it burned his eyes. "Isn't there anything else I can do?"

Her voice rose a notch. "Do you want to help or not?"

"All right. I'll chop the onion," he said resolutely. He walked around the island and stood beside her. She slid a cutting board towards him as he reached for a knife. "How do you want it chopped?"

"Diced in small pieces."

He placed the onion on the cutting board. "I can't guarantee that I'll do as good of a job as you, but I'll do my best." He cut off the end to remove the skin and began chopping. He heard her snigger. "What?"

"That's terrible. I'm amazed you haven't cut off your finger using a knife that way. Do it this way." She placed a mango on the cutting board in front of her and reached for another knife. "The front part goes down first, then rock the knife back in a smooth movement. Like so," she said, demonstrating on the mango. Her motions were swift and succinct.

"All right." He mimicked her movements. "How's that?" he asked a couple minutes later.

She nodded. "Much better."

They chopped in companionable silence. Fumes from the onion burned Chas's eyes. He let the crocodile tears flow freely down his cheeks as he looked at Ryleigh. "It's terrible," he lamented, faking a trembling voice.

"What?" she asked, concern flickering over her features.

He could tell she was trying to decide if he was really crying or if his eyes were just watering from the onion. "I never pictured you as a discriminatory person."

She blinked. "I'm not." She gave him a puzzled look, studying him. "Why would you say that?"

"You won't go out with me because I'm a football player ... and a celebrity." He sniffed, placing the knife down as he wiped the tears.

A startled laugh escaped her throat. "That's not true."

"Is so," he taunted softly, thinking how easy it would be to just kiss her again. He leaned forward slightly so that his face was level with hers. He could see her indecision as her mouth dissolved in a tight, colorless line.

Fire flashed from her eyes. "I'm not doing this with you."

Chas was used to dealing with pressure. He didn't give up easily and wasn't about to just let this go. "All right, then tell me why not."

A frigid silence descended between them as she reached for another mango and began furiously chipping away at it with her knife.

"Why were you so rattled by what Selena said?"

She went rigid.

"She was just jealous of you," Chas continued.

"That's absurd! Why would a woman like her be jealous of me?"

"Because you're beautiful." It cut to see the doubt in her eyes. How could Ryleigh not know that she was, not only, beautiful but the complete package? "You are beautiful," he repeated with certainty, hoping she'd realize he was speaking the truth. "Also, Selena could tell how much I like you."

She stopped chopping, blinking rapidly.

He touched her arm and was relieved when she didn't pull away. "Tell me about your past," he implored. "Was it your ex-husband who hurt you?"

Her eyes glittered with moisture.

"It's okay. You can tell me," he said in a smooth, comforting tone. He wanted Ryleigh to realize that he was safe. He'd never do anything intentionally to hurt her.

She let out a long sigh, her shoulders sagging. "Yes, Joey hurt me."

The burst of anger that stabbed through him took him by surprise. His jaw tightened. "What did he do?"

"Joey's a big kid who never grew up. He's charming and funny, but he has no concept of responsibility or what it means to be a parent. I realized that I couldn't count on him to be a provider or to look after Noah." She lifted her chin, her eyes going fierce. "I had to do it myself."

He digested all that she'd said. "So, was Joey abusive?"

She let out a harsh laugh. "No, not in the traditional sense. The biggest thing Joey ever did was destroy the dream I had built of the two of us." The words came out hard and bitter. She shrugged, giving him a sad smile. "We all start out having big dreams, but then we grow up."

"It doesn't have to be that way," he countered. "You can still dream." He gave her a searching look. "Dreams still can come true," he added.

Tears filled her eyes as she blinked to hold them back, looking away.

He got the feeling that there was more she wasn't telling him. "What else is holding you back?"

She huffed out a breath.

"Please, tell me everything so I'll understand."

For a second, he feared she might refuse, but then her jaw started working as she nodded. "It was hard to pick up the pieces after Joey and I divorced. Joey works in computers. He earns a good living ... when he's working, that is," she added, her tone hardening. "When Noah was little, I stayed home and took care of him."

"Makes sense."

"When Joey and I got divorced, I had no skills—no way to make a living. As I told you, I had just enrolled in cooking school, then found out I was pregnant with Noah, so I dropped out. Anyway, I had to find a way to make money, something I could do and still be at home with Noah. I'd always liked cooking, so it was a good fit."

"It seems like you're doing well with your business."

She hesitated. "Yeah, it has its ups and downs. I'd like to grow my client list."

"You've got me now." He grinned broadly and was relieved when she chuckled. Maybe his efforts to break the ice and get through to her were working.

"After I got over Joey, I built up the courage to start dating again." She paused, and he could tell she was trying to decide if she should tell him more.

"What happened?" he prompted.

A hard mask came over her features. "I thought I'd found a great guy. I let him into my life. Noah was crazy about him." She pushed out a brittle laugh. "As it turned out, he was married." Her voice grew intense. "I promised myself then that I would never again put myself or Noah in a compromising position. Noah must always come first," she said adamantly.

"Of course. I would never ask you to do anything else."

"Don't you see? There are no guarantees. You said so yourself. We don't know what will happen between us six months from now, or even two months from now, for that matter. You're a high-powered celebrity. You move in a totally different circle than I do." She gave him a pleading look. "Please try to understand. I have to do what's right for Noah."

"Okay, so don't bring Noah into it."

She made a face. "Huh?"

"We'll keep our relationship on the down low. We can give ourselves ... let's see ... four months. We should know by then if things will work out."

She giggled. "You're insane!"

"No, just hear me out. Every relationship I've ever had has gone great for the first four months. After that, things fall apart."

She arched an eyebrow. "It sounds like your track record is worse than mine. I was at least married to Joey for a couple of years before things starting falling apart."

He held up a finger. "Ah, but you had warning signs before that, right?"

"Yes, I suppose I did."

"Why didn't you heed them?"

She sucked in a deep breath. "Because I was stupid and blind. I thought I loved Joey enough to change him." She looked embarrassed.

"I understand. It happens." He looked her in the eye. "If we give ourselves four months, we'll know for sure."

The longing in her eyes evoked the same inside of him. He swallowed, trying to figure out how to persuade her. If he pushed too hard, she'd go the other direction. He offered a silent prayer, asking for help to know what to say. A memory flashed through his mind. He smiled inwardly. Of course. This would help Ryleigh understand. "Ever since I was a kid, I wanted to play football. When I was a sophomore in high school, I was the second-string running back for the varsity team. Clyde Manning, a senior, was the starting running back. He was agile and fast, so fast that I never thought I'd be able to catch him, much less vie for his position. We were in the playoffs when the unthinkable happened. There were two minutes left before halftime when Manning went down with a sprained ankle." A deep chuckle rumbled in his chest. "I'll never forget how petrified I was when I realized I would have to take his spot. I stumbled back to the field house with the rest of the team. All I could hear was the voice in my head, telling me I couldn't do it." He swallowed when Ryleigh's face drained to the color of his granite countertops. He suspected that similar voices played the same refrain in her head. His voice gathered intensity, practically reliving the event. "Everything was riding on this game. The winner would go on to state and play for a chance at the championship. I was sitting on a bench, my back against the lockers, staring down at the floor while the coach delivered his pep speech to the team."

"What happened?" she asked when he paused.

He smiled, remembering. "I glanced up and was shocked to see my dad standing just behind the coach. He'd left the stands and come to the field house."

Ryleigh's eyes popped. "Really? Why?"

"Dad waited until the coach finished, then politely asked if he could have a minute to speak to me." The coach reluctantly agreed. "Dad took me aside and said, 'Son, I know you're scared.'"

"Yes," I admitted, "I am."

"He gave me this crooked smile that's so my dad."

"Well, it must run in the family. I've seen that same crooked smile on you," Ryleigh inserted with a laugh.

"Really?" The admiration in her tone gave him pause.

"Really," she repeated. As their eyes met, a connection hummed in his chest. This thing with Ryleigh was getting stronger and stronger.

"What happened next?" she prompted, the eagerness in her eyes, turning them a rich emerald.

It thrilled him to know that he had her undivided attention. A smile tugged at his lips. "Dad looked me in the eye and said with all the confidence in the world, 'Son, you've only got one problem.'"

When he paused for effect, she gave him a playful shove. "Don't keep me in suspense."

"I'm sorry," he said bobbing his head from side-to-side, his voice monotone like an impersonal telephone operator. "What were we talking about?"

She growled. "Seriously?"

He held up a hand. "All right, all right. I'm getting to the good part." He paused again, looking her in the eye, enunciating every word. "My dad said, 'You're afraid of success. Stop being afraid of yourself. Just get out there and do what you were born to do.'"

Ryleigh's mouth parted, eyes larger than silver dollars. She put her hand to her throat, spreading her fingers out like a fan. "What did you do?"

"Just what my dad said. I went out and did what I'd wanted to do from the time I was a kid. We won the playoff and state championship." He felt a note of pride telling Ryleigh this.

She grew pensive. "I get the message," she said dryly. "You think I'm afraid."

He didn't back down in the slightest. "Yes, I do. You're afraid of the hypothetical."

Her brow creased. "What do you mean?"

"You're so worried about what could happen in the future that you're letting it hinder the present. I'm here. You're here." He grinned. "The two of us are dynamite together. You felt it when we kissed."

Her face went scarlet. "I plead the fifth," she uttered.

He winked. "That's okay. It's written all over your face."

She touched her cheeks, groaning. "How embarrassing."

"I find it charming." He caught her eyes. "I have a good feeling about us, Ryleigh. That's worth fighting for." Even as he spoke the words, a strong certainty flowed through him. He could tell from her expression that she felt it too. He cupped her cheek. "All I'm asking is that you keep our date on Friday. Go to dinner with me. See what happens." He held his breath, waiting for her answer. "Don't be afraid of success," he added softly, rubbing his thumb over her soft skin.

A tentative smile played on her lips, giving her an angelic glow. "All right."

He blinked. "Did you just say yes?"

She laughed. "Yes," she said loudly.

"Yes!" he exclaimed, pumping a fist in the air as he did a victory dance.

She sniggered out a laugh. "Well, I did say *yes* until I saw that." She wrinkled her forehead, crossing her arms over her chest. "Is that supposed to be dancing?"

"Hey!" he countered, pulling her into his arms as he made her dance with him.

"All right, Irish Flash," she said a minute later as she extricated herself from his arms. "Let me finish making this lunch before we both starve."

"You'll get no arguments from me there." His stomach rumbled. He reached to grab a handful of diced mangoes, but she swatted his hand.

"Don't do that," she scolded. "We won't have any left for the salsa."

"All right, Miss Bossy. Why don't I set the table?"

"Thank you," she said sweetly, batting her eyelashes. She was trying to be funny, but as her lashes brushed demurely against her high cheekbones, his stomach flipped. Ryleigh seemed oblivious to the effect she had on him. Maybe that was part of her appeal.

As Chas went to get the plates out of the cupboard, he felt like he'd scored a dozen touchdowns. No, this was even better because Ryleigh's heart was the ultimate win. A game he was prepared to spend a lifetime playing if it brought her to him in the end.

9

Four months for Chas and me to know if things are going to work. Ryleigh had been rolling that notion around in her head ever since Chas mentioned it. Four months with Chas O'Brien seemed like bliss. He was right. They would know by then if they could build a relationship together. She and Joey only dated two months before he proposed. She'd been so in love with him that she accepted his proposal on the spot. They were married one month later. It wasn't until afterwards, when the excitement wore off, that Ryleigh started seeing things in Joey that were concerning. Had she been more cautious, she might've seen those things before she took the leap. She tightened her hold on the steering wheel. No, she couldn't think like that. Their marriage had brought her Noah. She'd relive an infinite number of failed marriages to get her beautiful son.

Then again, this wasn't about Joey or Noah. This was about the future. Her thoughts went to Dylan Ellis. She'd only known him a mere three weeks before she invited him into her home to have dinner with her and Noah. Tess had been leery of Dylan from day one. "He has shifty eyes," she said.

Ryleigh had attributed Tess's misgivings to her overprotective nature. She chuckled. Tess was fiercely loyal, the best sister Ryleigh could ever ask for. Sure, the two of them got on each other's nerves occasionally, but when the chips were down, they knew they could depend on one another. Loyalty was something Ryleigh would never take for granted. Her jaw tightened thinking of her flighty mother who'd deserted her husband and daughters without a second thought. She'd gone on a crusade to "find herself." That discovery led her to the panhandle of Florida where she waitressed at a bar that allowed her to sing on stage for customers on the weekends. She'd been divorced three times. The last Ryleigh heard, she was living with her boyfriend, a man a decade younger who owned a surf shop.

To his credit, Ryleigh's dad stuck around, but he was so torn up over his wife leaving that he could hardly function. For a solid year, he got up and went to work. Then, he'd come home and say a couple quick words to Ryleigh and Tess before sequestering himself in his bedroom. He even went so far as to put a mini-fridge and microwave in his bedroom so he wouldn't have to come out to get food. A year later, he married Carol a secretary at the boot manufacturing plant where he worked as a quality assurance manager. At first Carol seemed wonderful. Ryleigh and Tess were elated because she coaxed their dad out of his shell. He became part of the family, started laughing again. Carol would come over and make dinner, complete with homemade chocolate chip cookies. Desperate for a mother's influence in their lives, Ryleigh and Tess welcomed Carol with open arms.

After the wedding, Carol moved into the house. Shortly thereafter, things began to shift. Carol became maniacal about keeping things clean. Also, she was miserly, hoarding every penny their father earned. Ryleigh and Tess couldn't even throw away a used Ziploc bag without getting the third degree from Carol. When it came time to buy school clothes, Carol took the girls to yard sales rather than regular stores. Also, Carol was territorial over their dad's time, viewing Ryleigh and Tess as competition.

When Carol had a child of her own, Ryleigh and Tess were swept by the wayside as all their dad and Carol's energy went into Mikey, who was named after their dad. Mikey grew up spoiled rotten.

Ryleigh and Tess loved their half-brother, but there was always a division between them. Mikey was now a teenager. Ryleigh's dad, Carol, and Mikey lived a short distance across town, but it was rare that Ryleigh and Tess went to visit.

Splatters of rain on the windshield caught Riley's attention as she turned on her wipers. She peered through the windshield. Her headlights were long, cylindrical haloes pushing through the moisture of the dark, inky air. She let her mind get lost in the monotony of the wipers as she turned onto her street. The road glistened with a coat of the newly fallen rain, making everything look fresh and untouched.

She sighed, an unconscious smile curving her lips as she thought about Chas. Maybe he was right. Deep down, she was afraid of success. No, not exactly. She was afraid to believe that good things could actually happen to her. Yet, good things were happening. She was getting the chance to participate in the mother of all cooking competitions. Even better than that, she had a wonderful man in her life who, for some reason she still couldn't fathom, was crazy about her. Her skin swirled with warmth thinking of the long, drugging kiss he'd given her before he opened her car door and helped her inside. She'd looked in the rearview mirror as she drove away, caught the flicker of his wide, reckless smile as he waved goodbye.

Four months. She'd take things one step at a time. If all went as well as she hoped, she could ease Chas into Noah's life. She frowned. There was still the problem of Chas's celebrity status. People noticed him wherever he went. Today in the grocery store, after the run-in with the notorious Selena Simpson, three people had stopped them. An older man wanted Chas's autograph for his grandsons. Two women gushed about how they couldn't believe they'd actually met Chas. They jabbered on for what seemed like an eternity before asking if they could take selfies with him. Chas was gracious, but Ryleigh could tell he was uncomfortable with all the attention. Heck, she was uncomfortable with it too! How long would it take for the media to get wind of the fact that they were dating? A shiver ran down her spine. That couldn't happen. They had to be careful and stay out of the limelight. Was she a fool to even risk getting involved with Chas? As she pulled into her driveway and parked underneath the carport, she took in a deep breath, trying to calm her nerves.

She'd felt good about giving her and Chas a chance. She couldn't let her fears overrule her good sense. Just thinking those words helped restore a sense of calm. It was a little after nine pm. Ryleigh appreciated Tess taking care of Noah tonight. Tess moving into the house had been a tremendous blessing for all involved. She paid a portion of the mortgage and was a second mother to Noah. Someday, when either Ryleigh or Tess got married, it would be a huge adjustment to separate their households.

Ryleigh got out of the car and went inside, entering through the side door that led to the kitchen. "Hello, I'm home." She didn't want to say it too loud in case Noah was already asleep. His bedtime was eight thirty, but the little stinker routinely pushed to stay up longer. While Ryleigh was more of a stickler for the rules, Tess usually gave in, letting him get away with too much. Ryleigh deposited her purse and keys on the table. The faint scent of food lingered in the air. The kitchen was sparkling clean, a dish towel draped over the handle of the oven. Again, Ryleigh was immensely grateful for Tess.

"In here," Tess said.

Ryleigh found her in the living room, curled up on the couch, watching a movie. She halted in her tracks, a twinge of alarm jabbing her in the gut when she saw the tears pooling in Tess's eyes. "What's wrong?" Ryleigh's throat tightened as she swallowed.

Tears slipped down Tess's cheeks as she gulped out a squeaky laugh. "*An Affair to Remember.*"

Relief swelled through Ryleigh as she smiled. "One of my favorites."

Tess sniffed, wiping her nose. She held out the remote and pushed pause. "Every time I see it, I bawl like a baby."

"Me too," Ryleigh chuckled. She plopped down beside Tess and kicked off her shoes. "Which part are you on?" She looked at the TV screen. "Ah, the climax." Debra Kerr was sitting on the couch, a white shawl draped over her shoulders. Cary Grant had just realized she was paralyzed. "Don't let me keep you from watching the end."

Tess used her palms to wipe away the remaining tears as she sucked in a large sniffle, rubbing her hands up and down in fast motions against her pajama pants. "It's okay. I'll finish it later." An impish grin tugged at her lips. "Right now, I want to hear all about your day. The last time I saw you, it seemed like y'all were getting along just fine."

Blotches crawled up Ryleigh's neck as her hand clutched her throat. "Yeah, it went well."

Tess shifted, drawing her leg tighter up underneath her. "Go ahead. Spill it," she ordered, shoving Ryleigh's arm.

Ryleigh chuckled. "All right. I will. First, how did it go with Noah?"

"Great." Tess made a face. "Well, except for the homework. *Sheesh.* That's a lot of homework for a second grader. Made me want to hunt down the wretched teacher who assigned it and make her do it!"

"I know. It's a lot. Did you get it all done?"

"Yeah, finally. We went over Noah's spelling words too."

"Oh, good."

"He's got some hard words this week. *Location* and *cubicle*. Really? For a second grader? Ridiculous," she scoffed.

"Were those his challenge words?"

"Yeah, but still." She rolled her eyes.

"What did you make for dinner?"

"Mac and cheese and fish sticks."

Ryleigh bunched her brows. "Really? You couldn't come up with anything better than that?"

"It's what Noah wanted," Tess said defensively. She thrust out her lower lip. "Also, I was tired from cooking all day at Gemma's."

"I really appreciate your help today. Is Noah asleep?"

"Well, he's in bed, but I'm not sure he's asleep yet." Her eyebrow shot up. "I'm sure he'll come running when he realizes you're home."

Ryleigh didn't really mind. It would be good to see Noah. "I'll go check on him in a few minutes." She thought of something else. "How did it go at Gemma's?"

Tess's countenance brightened. "Great." She chuckled. "That

woman's a character. She was telling me all about how she and Doug met. Then she broke out the family album."

Ryleigh's eyes widened. "Oh, no. She didn't."

"Yes, she did," Tess asserted. "You know, Gemma's an attractive lady now, but she was quite the dish when she was younger. Doug was cute too."

"Really?" An image of Doug flashed through Ryleigh's mind. Portly with dusty hair, receding on top. His jovial smile was his best feature. Still, she couldn't imagine that he'd ever been attractive.

"I know, crazy, huh?" Tess laughed. "Anyway, everything went well. I prepared all the usual meals." She pulled a face. "We really should mix it up a little."

"Believe me," Ryleigh said dourly, "I've tried. Gemma insists on having the same thing every week. Lasagna, chicken enchiladas …"

"Pot roast, meatloaf and scalloped potatoes," Tess finished. "I've got it down pat." She sighed, waving a hand. "All right. Enough about that. Tell me about Chas."

"Things are good," Ryleigh answered evasively.

A rich laugh rumbled in her throat as she tossed her long hair. "Oh, no. You're not getting off with that. I want the juicy details."

Ryleigh laughed. "All right. Guess who Chas and I saw at the grocery store?"

"The tooth fairy?" Tess joked.

"The tooth fairy would've been better." Ryleigh paused.

Tess looked like she was about to burst. "Who?" she exploded.

"Selena Simpson, Chas's ex-girlfriend."

"No!" Tess's eyes grew rounder than two full moons. "The leggy model we saw online?"

"Yep." Distaste filled Ryleigh's mouth.

"What happened?"

Ryleigh chuckled dryly. "Well, as you can imagine, it didn't take long for the claws to come out."

"Yours or hers?" Tess asked with a wicked laugh.

"Hers. She told me to enjoy it while it lasted—with Chas—that he'd find my replacement soon enough." The animosity came rushing back with a vengeance.

Sparks shot from Tess's eyes. "Are you serious? She had the nerve to say that?"

"Yep."

"What did you say?"

"Nothing. It took me off guard."

Tess's eyes narrowed to slits. "I can think of a thing or two that I would've said."

"Yes, I'm sure you would have." Ryleigh felt grudging admiration for her feisty younger sister. Afterwards, Ryleigh had thought of a dozen witty comebacks she should've used, but she'd never been that quick on her feet.

"What happened next?" Tess asked impatiently.

"We went back to Chas's house. I started preparing lunch." When she hesitated, Tess paddled her hand in a circular motion.

"And?"

Ryleigh was tempted to hold back, but that would be futile because Tess would eventually wheedle it out of her. Also, Tess was a great sounding board. Ryleigh wanted to hear why Tess thought Chas was so great. "Maybe I should check on Noah, before I launch into all this."

"No, don't keep me hanging. Noah's fine."

"If I wait too long, he'll be asleep." She stopped when she saw the sheepish look on Tess's face. "What's going on?"

"Well …" Tess hedged "… Noah was having a hard time getting to sleep, so I told him he could watch *Sponge Bob Square Pants* on my iPad."

"Tess! He has school tomorrow."

"I know, but what's the difference between him watching something and lying there, staring at the ceiling? At least now he's occupied, instead of asking for a drink of water and piece of bread every few minutes."

A giggle rose in Ryleigh's throat. Noah often complained of being hungry at night, mostly so he wouldn't have to go to bed. The rule was that he could have a slice of bread and water. It had become sort of a tradition for Noah to have the bread and water before bed. "All right. I'll tell you the highlights and then I'd better put Noah to bed, for real. Otherwise, he'll be impossible to get up in the morning." She dipped her head sideways, trying to decide what to share first. "Seeing Selena Simpson." Her jaw tensed. "Well, it made me start having second thoughts about Chas."

Tess's jaw dropped. "No! Don't say that."

Ryleigh put a hand on Tess's leg. "Don't worry, Chas talked me off the ledge."

"Oh, good," Tess breathed.

Ryleigh studied her younger sister. "You really like him, don't you?"

"Yes, I do."

"Why?"

Tess played with a strand of her hair, twisting it around her index finger. "Well, aside from the fact that he's a hot football player, he's really nice." Her features softened, sincerity shining in her eyes. "The two of you are good together."

"We are?" A smile tugged at Ryleigh's lips. "Yes, we are," she said decisively. The admission spread like warm butter through her. "I really like him a lot."

"I know you do."

"I guess that's what scares me." Her voice quivered slightly. "I can't afford to make another mistake."

Tess put a hand over hers. "You won't, sis."

The certainty in Tess's eyes confused Ryleigh. "How can you be so sure? I thought everything was great with Joey and then Dylan." Her chest tightened. "Only to have everything blow up in my face. Who's to say that won't happen again?"

"Chas isn't like Joey or Dylan. He's a good guy."

"How can you be so sure?" Her tongue started moving a mile a minute. "We haven't known him long enough to make that determination. Sure, he seems great now, but he's bound to have his flaws."

"Of course he does," Tess interrupted. She gave Ryleigh a perceptive look. "So, do you."

The comment came at Ryleigh like a punch in the gut. She pressed her lips together, swallowing. Yes, she had faults. Plenty.

"One of your faults is that you freak out when anything good happens to you."

Ryleigh tensed. "That's not fair," she countered, even though she'd just thought the same thing on the drive home.

"Yes, it is, and you know it." Tess lifted her chin, eyes blazing with the self-assured knowledge that she was speaking the truth. "Even on a sunny day with white, puffy clouds floating in the sky, you look for that one cloud with the dark underlining."

Tears pressed against Ryleigh's eyes. "How can I not?" she squeaked.

Tess's expression took on a tender touch. "It's okay to have fears ... as long as you don't let those fears take over your life."

A wretched tear escaped, trickling down her cheek. Ryleigh hurriedly brushed it away. "How do you know Chas is a good guy?" She heard the desperation in her own voice, knew she was craving validation.

"Well, for starters Gemma says he is."

"Really?" That was encouraging. Yes, of course Gemma thought he was a good guy. If she hadn't, she wouldn't have wanted to fix Ryleigh up with him. "Why does Gemma think highly of Chas?" She cleared her throat. "Did she tell you anything specific?" She was dangling on the edge of a cliff here, her fingers frantically gripping for something to hold onto, something to keep her from going over the edge.

Tess tipped her head, looking thoughtful. "Actually, she told me a few things."

Ryleigh leaned forward, intent on catching every word.

"Chas belongs to an outreach program, a big brother type thing where he acts as a mentor to troubled youth."

She frowned. "Chas didn't mention that."

"Probably because he doesn't like to brag about himself."

"Hmm ... that's impressive."

"Yes, it is. Also, he's helped Doug with home repairs a few times. Gemma said that just last week he came outside and saw Doug up on a ladder, trying to find the source of a leak around their chimney. Chas went up and helped. Also, Chas gets along great with Gemma's grandkids. He comes over and throws the football with them when they're in town. That may seem like a little thing, but it's often the little things that clue you in to the real person."

"I agree." She pursed her lips. "That's probably why Gemma wanted to buy a football for Noah, because she was used to Chas spending time with her grandkids."

"Probably."

Tess scoped her with an intuitive eye. "At the end of the day, it really doesn't matter what Gemma or I think of Chas. It's what you think." She paused. "What does your gut tell you?"

Ryleigh pondered the question. "That he's a good guy." Even as she spoke the words, her heart leapt as a blanket of warmth flowed over her. "He's a good guy," she proclaimed exuberantly. "I feel it."

Tess reached for her hands, squeezing them. "Yes, he is. You deserve all the good that's coming your way. Don't run from it."

"Don't be afraid of success," Ryleigh said, a smile tugging at her lips.

"Exactly!" Tess boomed, looking impressed. Her eyes shimmered. "Where's Chas taking you to dinner Friday night?"

Ryleigh laughed, feeling deliriously happy. "That's the best part. He's taking me to a Mexican restaurant called *Los Tios*."

The corners of Tess's lips turned down. "I thought he'd take you someplace nicer." She shrugged. "I mean, the food there is excellent." She spread her hands. "I'm just saying ..."

"Chas's taking me there for a reason." Excitement built inside her chest, and she couldn't stop the large grin from spilling over her lips.

"What?" Tess asked dubiously.

"The restaurant is owned by Ace Sanchez's family."

Tess's expression remained blank.

"You don't know who he is?"

"Nope," Tess snipped, folding her arms over her chest as she eyed Ryleigh. Tess didn't like feeling like anyone else had the upper hand or knew more than she did.

Laughter pealed out of Ryleigh's lips. "Yeah, I didn't recognize the name either. Chas had to spell it out for me." A lock of hair fell over her eye as she pushed it away. "Ace played for the Titans. He and his wife Silver own several restaurants. Silver started out as an event planner."

Tess's eyes sparked with enthusiasm as her voice rose an octave. "Wow."

"Chas is going to introduce me to Silver. He thinks she'll be a good connection. Hopefully, it'll land us some more clients. Also, I want to pick her brain about what it takes to open a restaurant."

"That's awesome!"

"I know."

"See? You already know Chas is a great guy. You just wanted to hear me say it, didn't you?"

"Yeah." Ryleigh offered a docile grin. "Sorry, I guess I just needed some positive reinforcement."

"Well, you've got it," Tess said heartily. "That's so nice of Chas to introduce you to Silver Sanchez. That could be huge."

"I know."

Tess's eyes danced with excitement. "Ooh, you're somebody now," she cooed. "Hobnobbing with the movers and shakers. Just don't forget the little people, okay?"

Ryleigh lightly shoved her arm. "Yeah right."

"Seriously, sis. I'm glad so many good things are happening." She hesitated. "It makes it easier to tell you the bad news."

"What?" Ryleigh braced herself for whatever was coming.

"Mary cancelled for tomorrow."

"All right. That's not the end of the world. Did she reschedule?"

"No, she's not gonna be able to use our services anymore."

Ryleigh's muscles pulled taut. "Why not?"

"She can't afford it. Her husband just lost his job."

"Wow. I hate that for Mary."

"I know. I hate it for us too," Tess said glumly. "We need the money."

Ryleigh's head spun. Bills were stacking up. Business had been booming during Christmas, to the point where she and Tess could hardly keep up. However, January had been slow. It was like someone turned off the water faucet. "All right," she said to herself, trying to think. "Losing one client's not the end of the world. Gemma is paying us extra. Also, Chas is paying me too." She'd not planned to charge Chas for her time, only for the cost of ingredients. Now, however, seeing as how things had changed, she'd get him to pay her usual fee. "That should more than make up for what we'll lose with Mary."

Tess's lips formed a grim line. "It gets worse, I'm afraid."

"What do you mean?" Ryleigh's lungs shrank to the size of peas making it hard to get a good breath.

"We also lost Sheri Wilson."

Ryleigh's tongue felt like lead as she pushed the question out. "In the same day?"

"Yep."

The worry carved over Tess's features heightened her own apprehension. She rubbed her forehead. "Why?"

"Her daughter got accepted into a private academy. The tuition's costing them a fortune, so they're having to conserve."

Ryleigh furrowed her brows. "In January? I thought schools started in the fall."

"Evidently, this one had a slot open up and Sheri's daughter was on the waiting list."

A humorless laugh rumbled in Ryleigh's chest. "I guess I'm gonna have to win the Grilling and Chilling contest now," she said lightly, feeling as though the walls were closing in around her.

Tess touched her arm, giving her a reassuring smile. "It'll work out. If I have to, I'll pick up a part-time job on the side."

"I had hoped the online advertising would give us a boost." Ryleigh looked at Tess. "Do you think it's helping at all?" She hated the desperation in her voice.

"I don't know." Tess let out a long sigh. "I'll look at everything in the morning."

A glum silence settled between them.

"Sorry to lay that all on you tonight," Tess finally said. "I just thought you'd wanna know."

"Yes, I do. I'm glad you told me." Her shoulders ached from tension. She rubbed her neck. "We'll think of something," she said, forcing a smile at Tess.

"Maybe Silver Sanchez can give you some great leads," Tess offered hopefully.

"That would be great," Ryleigh agreed. She stood. "Well, I guess I'd better check on Noah."

"Oh, I almost forgot to tell you. Joey stopped by tonight."

"How's he doing?" Ryleigh asked mechanically, her mind still on the business, or lack thereof.

Tess's expression turned sour. "You know Joey. Same as always." A wicked glint lit her eyes. "He was agitated that you weren't here, especially when he realized you were with Chas."

Ryleigh's gut tightened like a washcloth being wrung out to dry. "Tess," she began with a heavy sigh, "were you needling Joey about me dating?"

Tess lifted her chin. "If you mean was I reminding Joey of what a dope he was for shirking his responsibilities and losing the greatest thing he ever had, then the answer is *yes*."

Ryleigh rubbed a hand over her forehead. "No good can come of that."

"Why do you care what Joey thinks?" Tess flung back.

"I don't care, except for the fact that he's my son's father." She lowered her voice. "Joey and I are in a good place right now. Let's not rock the boat."

"You sure about the friend thing?" Tess asked with an arched eyebrow. She let out a trill of deviant giggles. "Joey about wet his pants when I asked him if he'd mind watching Noah this Friday while you go out on your date."

"Tess!" Ryleigh let out a shaky laugh. "Was Joey okay with it?"

"No, not really. But he agreed to it. I figured you'd have a hard time broaching the topic with good ole' Joey, so I did it for you. You can thank me later."

Admittedly, Ryleigh was kind of glad Tess had taken matters into her own hands and saved Ryleigh from an awkward situation.

Tess shook her head. "You know, to have come from such a great family, Joey didn't amount to much, did he?"

"Careful," Ryleigh warned, "Noah might hear you."

Tess continued as if Ryleigh hadn't spoken. "Natalie is one of my closest friends. It's hard to believe she and Joey are siblings."

Ryleigh was used to Tess bagging on Joey. Most of the time, Ryleigh let it go in one ear and out the other. Tonight, however, with worry over the business looming, Tess's words rubbed Ryleigh the wrong way. "Why're you so down on Joey all the time?"

Tess threw back her head, her nostrils flaring. "Why're you defending him?"

"I'm not!"

Tess snorted. "You know what that loser had the nerve to ask me?"

"What?" Ryleigh asked dully. A headache was spreading behind her eyes. With every beat of her pulse, she felt a stab of pain.

"If I thought you'd let him move back in."

For a second, Ryleigh thought she'd heard wrong. "Huh?"

"Yeah, the loser wants to move back in." Tess grew animated, her hands flying as she talked. "I told him it would be a cold day in—"

"Mom!"

Ryleigh turned as Noah scuttled in and gave her a bear hug. "I missed you." He buried his head in her waist.

"I missed you too, sport," she said, ruffling his hair. "Were you good for Tess?"

"Uh, huh."

"He was good," Tess affirmed.

"It's getting late. You need to get some sleep, so you'll feel good tomorrow."

He held her tight. Then he lifted his head, peering up at her. His lower lip jiggled loosely, tears pooling in his big, brown eyes.

Confusion swirled through Ryleigh. "What's wrong?"

Noah's mouth worked until finally, he spit it out. "Are you gonna leave with the football player?"

Ice flowed through Ryleigh's veins. "What?" Dizziness tumbled over her. "Where did you hear that?" Her head felt like it would split in two as her eyes flew to Tess's.

Tess spread her hands. "Don't look at me. I would never say anything like that." Her eyes narrowed. "But I know who would."

Joey! Ryleigh's mind shouted. She felt like a thousand needles were pricking her all at once. Somehow, she managed to find her voice. "Where did you hear that?"

Noah looked down at the floor.

"Noah?" Gently, she pushed him back and placed her hand under his chin, lifting his face. "Who told you that?"

"I dunno," he answered haltingly.

Ryleigh looked at Tess whose face was masked with outrage. Her gaze went back to Noah as she fought to keep the anger out of her voice. "Did your dad say that to you?"

Silence.

Her throat had constricted to the size of a straw. She swallowed, trying to clear it. "It's okay. You can tell me," she began in a gentle tone. "Was it your dad?"

Noah's face crumbled as he burst into tears. She let him cry for a moment, stroking his head. "It's okay," she soothed.

His shoulders shook, muffled sobs issuing from his throat.

"Of course it was Joey," Tess muttered, balling a fist. "Who else could it be?"

Ryleigh rubbed circles over Noah's back. "Honey, was it Daddy who told you that?"

Finally, after what seemed to be an interminable about of time, Noah lifted his head. "Yes," he squeaked. He shrank back, his head lowering into his shoulders. "Daddy said you'd be mad if I told you," he said timidly.

"I'm not mad at you sweetheart." Ryleigh got down on one knee and looked him in the eye. "No, I'm not leaving with a football player or anyone else." Anger punched through her veins like a Taser. Had Joey been here, she would've told him off, then slapped him a few times across the jaw. She looked Noah in the eye. "I will never leave you … for anyone." She grasped his arm in a firm grip, but not too hard for fear of hurting him. She squared her jaw. "Do you understand?"

He nodded, biting his lower lip.

"I mean that. You are my son." Tears gathered in Ryleigh's eyes as she looked at her beautiful boy. "You are the greatest thing that's ever happened to me." Her voice caught. "I'll never leave you for anyone," she said fiercely. "I'm going to be right here by your side, watching you grow up. Okay?"

He nodded.

She touched his face. "I love you."

He smiled in relief. "I love you too." She pulled him in for a tight hug, breathing in his scent of bubble bath and wheat bread. It burned her to the core that Joey would plant seeds of doubts in Noah. Joey knew how devastating it had been for Ryleigh when her mom left. He also knew how hard she'd tried to create a protective environment for Noah so he wouldn't have to go through what she had. How dare Joey use her son to manipulate her!

She stood, feeling weary to the bone. "Let's get you to bed, kiddo," she said in a light tone, belying her searing anger. She looked at Tess whose eyes were also burning like a tiger about to go on the rampage. "Let's talk about it later. After I get Noah to bed." She gave Tess a meaningful look. "Noah's had enough excitement for one day."

Tess nodded, clamping her mouth shut.

"I heard you had a good time with Tess," Ryleigh said to Noah in an upbeat, motherly tone. He jabbered out a response, but Ryleigh barely heard a word as she led Noah to bed. Tomorrow couldn't come soon enough. She was going to tell Joey exactly what she thought of his little stunt.

10

"Good morning, ladies," Joey said breezily as he strolled into the home office. Tess sparked wrath like she was a second away from jumping down Joey's throat, but Ryleigh gave her a warning look, telling her to keep her lips zipped. It was Ryleigh's place to jump down Joey's throat. No, she wasn't going to just jump down his throat. She was going to reach in and pull out his voice box.

The corners of Joey's lips drooped down as he looked back and forth between Tess and Ryleigh. His gaze settled on Ryleigh as he took his usual spot on the loveseat and propped his ankle on top of his thigh. He clasped his hands. "What's up?"

The accusation rushed out of Ryleigh like a whirlwind, nearly knocking the breath out of her. "Did you tell Noah that I was going to run away with a football player?"

Joey drew back. "What?" He let out a nervous laugh. "No."

"Liar!" Tess seethed, gripping the arms of her chair.

The whites of Joey's eyes popped, the corners of his jaws twitching. "Where's all of this animosity coming from?"

Ryleigh scooted forward in her seat, her back going ramrod

straight. "When I got home last night, Noah asked me if I was going to run away with a football player."

Joey laughed. "Really?" He rubbed his jaw. "That's a kid for you, huh?" he said blithely.

"No, that wasn't something a kid would come up with." Ryleigh spat out the words. "How dare you put doubts in Noah's mind!" Her voice shook with fury. "Especially considering my history with my mother."

Joey uncrossed his legs. He sat up, holding up his hands. "Hold it." His voice hardened. "I don't know where this is coming from, but I did not tell Noah that." He looked at Ryleigh, his dark eyes pleading. "I swear to you." He placed a hand over his chest. "You've gotta believe me, Ry."

Confusion trickled down Ryleigh's spine.

"He's lying," Tess growled. "Where else would Noah have heard something like that?" She eyed Joey. "I knew you were low, but I didn't think you were that low," she muttered.

Joey pushed out a haughty laugh. "Maybe you're the one who told Noah that."

Blood rushed to Tess's face. "I would never say anything like that. I'm glad Ryleigh's dating a good guy. You're just jealous because she found someone who's not afraid to step up to the plate and be a man."

The veins on Joey's neck bulged. For a second, Ryleigh feared he might jump up and punch Tess. His breathing was heavy and ragged. Then, he seemed to gain control of his emotions as he popped his knuckles, a strained smile stretching over his lips. "This is all a big misunderstanding."

When both sisters remained silent, he continued, addressing his words to Ryleigh. "Noah asked where you were. I told him you were out with a football player. He must've misunderstood."

"No, I think Noah understood exactly what you meant for him to understand," Tess said, the accusation in her voice unmistakable.

Joey grunted. "Are you gonna sit there and let your sister talk to me that way?" he asked Ryleigh. The look on his face was one of disbelief.

Varying emotions tumbled through Ryleigh. She was angry, disappointed, disillusioned, hurt. The words came out hoarse between her clenched teeth. "How could you resort to using our son as a tool to manipulate me? I thought we were friends."

"We are friends," Joey said loudly. He swore, then his eyes darkened with something Ryleigh couldn't discern as his voice grew persuasive. "Ry, we're more than friends." He swallowed, his Adam's apple moving up and down like it was connected to a pulley. "Losing you is the biggest regret of my life."

"Oh, please," Tess sneered. "Now she's supposed to feel sorry for you, because you couldn't measure up? Poor, Joey," she taunted in a soft, sing-song tone. "Never can hold down a job. The big, bad boss always gets in the way."

Anger flashed in Joey's eyes. "Enough!"

The outburst strangled the sisters into silence.

Joey rubbed his hands on his jeans, speaking in a hushed, controlled voice. "I made a mistake." His voice hitched as he brought a fist to his mouth, his handsome face clouding. "If I could go back and do it again, I would. I realize that time has passed, however."

Ryleigh's shoulders relaxed. "Yes, it has." The words spilled out between them like milk that could never again be returned to the carton. For a minute there, she feared that Joey was trying to get her back. That would've been a huge disaster. Thank goodness, he seemed to realize that whatever they once had was in the past. Joey seemed larger than life back then, able to talk her into almost anything with his silver tongue and uncommonly good looks. Now, however, he seemed like a small, vain man still holding onto the fragments of the past. She wished him well and wanted him to get on with his life—a life that involved her as little as possible.

"We can be friends," Joey continued.

"Friends don't manipulate each other," Tess fumed.

"Noah's a kid," Joey said easily, a quick boyish smile tumbling over his lips. "He misunderstood the situation."

"Yeah, right," Tess harrumphed.

Joey shot Tess a hard look. Then, he focused on Ryleigh, as if he were dismissing Tess altogether. "Ryleigh, I told Tess that I'd watch Noah Friday night while you go on your date. Consider it a peace offering."

Ryleigh didn't believe for one minute that Noah misunderstood the situation, but in Joey's defense Tess had baited him by rubbing his nose in the knowledge that Ryleigh was going out with Chas. Still, that was no excuse for Joey to behave as he had. Did she even trust Joey to watch Noah? He was Noah's father, after all. Even so, she hadn't been able to trust Joey to watch Noah when he was two. Maybe she shouldn't trust him now. How could she enjoy herself on a date wondering what rubbish Joey was putting into Noah's impressionable head?

"We'll have to see," she said evasively. Disappointment lodged heavily in her chest, knowing she'd have to cancel her date. Noah came first and that was that.

"No, we won't see," Tess snapped. "I'll watch Noah."

Ryleigh turned to her younger sister in surprise. "What about your date?"

"I'll reschedule."

"Thank you," Ryleigh breathed. Gratitude rose in her chest. She'd never been prouder to call Tess her sister. "I really appreciate you doing that."

Tess's eyes softened as she nodded.

Joey held up his hands again. "All right. I get it. I'm the enemy here. That's fine." His eyes misted as they locked with Ryleigh's. "Regardless of whatever you think of me, I swear to you that I'll never flake out on you again. I'll be there for you, through thick and thin."

"What a nice friend you are," Tess cooed in a mocking tone.

Joey ignored Tess. "When the thing with the football player runs its course, I'll be here." His voice rose to a crescendo.

Ryleigh gurgled a laugh. "You're so sure that it won't work out? I hate to disappoint you, but you're wrong." The calm certainty in her tone surprised her. It was good to know that the fuzziness in her brain over Chas was starting to clear. He was a good guy, and she wasn't going to miss out on her chance for happiness.

"No, that's not what I meant," Joey stammered, color fanning his face. "If it doesn't work out, I'll be here. That's what I meant to say." He gave her a beseeching look. "I just want you to be happy."

Tess's derisive laughter ricocheted around the room as she clapped slowly. "That was quite the performance. Bravo!"

Ryleigh wasn't sure what to make of this whole thing. Above all, she didn't want to make an enemy out of her son's father. She'd loved Joey once, enough for pity to crowd out any malice she felt for him. "Thanks," she said numbly. She gave Joey a wan smile. "All right. We need to get back to work. We've got a busy day."

"Oh, okay." Joey's voice rattled as he stood. "I guess I'll go then." He gave Ryleigh a dejected look. "Bye." He stepped up to her and leaned in, planting a kiss on her cheek. "See ya around." A fleeting smile touched his lips, but it didn't quite reach his wounded eyes.

When he left, he took the oppressive cloud of darkness with him.

"Finally!" Tess exclaimed. Her jaw tightened as she gave Ryleigh a significant look. "Thank your lucky stars that you're rid of him."

"Yes," Ryleigh agreed, breathing a sigh of relief. "Onto bigger and better things," she said under her breath.

Amusement lit Tess's eyes. "Amen. Like Chas O'Brien."

"Like Chas O'Brien," she repeated, realizing more than ever before that she was hopeful for her future. Maybe the third time really was the charm.

11

"You look fabulous," Tess said, her eyes flickering over Ryleigh with admiration.

"You don't think the dress is too much?" Ryleigh made a face, critically studying her reflection in the full-length mirror as she ran a self-conscious hand over her stomach. "It's so red and fitting." She tugged at the center section of the dress.

"Stop, or you'll stretch the fabric," Tess protested with a laugh. "That's the point. You look like a million bucks. You should wear red more often." She flashed a cheeky grin. "And, it doesn't hurt that you have on my dress."

Ryleigh patted her curls. "My hair's too big, isn't it? My lipstick too red." Her empty stomach churned acid. She'd been so keyed up about tonight's date that she'd forgotten to eat. Her body was reminding her of that full force now, but it was too late to do anything about it. She was meeting Chas at his house and riding with him to Los Tios. If she didn't leave in the next few minutes, she'd be late.

"I think you look pretty, Mom," Noah said, jumping up and down on Ryleigh's bed.

"Thanks," Ryleigh answered, turning to face him, her expression stern. "You know better than to jump on the bed."

Immediately, he plopped down, cross-legged. "Oops." A look passed between Noah and Tess. "She caught me," he said, laughter sparkling in his lively eyes.

Ryleigh couldn't help but laugh as her hand went to her hip. "I sense a conspiracy here. Do you jump on the bed while I'm gone?"

Noah looked wide-eyed at Tess, as if trying to figure out how to answer the question. Tess mouthed *no*. When she realized Ryleigh had seen her, she pulled a face. "What's so bad about jumping on the bed?" she huffed. "We used to do it."

"You used to jump on the bed?" Noah asked in amazement.

"Yes, but I shouldn't have," Ryleigh answered, shooting Tess an annoyed look. "You're teaching him bad habits."

"No, I'm not," Tess countered. "We're just having a little fun."

Ryleigh sighed, knowing there was no winning this argument. "I suppose there are worse things than jumping on the bed," she relented. "As long as you don't fall and bust your head open," she warned.

"I'll be careful," Noah assured her.

"Oh, and it's better to jump on Aunt Tess's bed instead of mine." Ryleigh got a kick out of Tess's mortified expression. "Hers has a better bounce."

"Thanks a lot," Tess said smartly.

Ryleigh blew her a kiss. "You're welcome. I figure it's better for your bed to be the collateral damage, instead of mine."

Noah wrinkled his nose. "What's collateral damage?"

Both Ryleigh and Tess laughed. "I'll let Aunt Tess explain it to you."

Noah hopped up on his knees. "Are you going on a date with Chas?" he asked tentatively.

Ryleigh rocked back. "You know who Chas is?"

Noah rolled his eyes. "Duh, I met him at Miss Gemma's house." Excitement sounded in his voice. "Chas is gonna throw the football with me. Miss Gemma and Mr. Doug bought me a really good football." His eyes grew pleading. "Will you ask him when he can throw the football?" He put his hands together. "Please?" he begged.

Ryleigh ruffled his hair. "You bet." She looked at Tess. "So much for keeping my relationship on the down low."

Tess shrugged. "Well, you've got a smart son. He knows something's up."

"What's up?" Noah asked, bouncing on his knees.

Ryleigh sat down on the edge of the bed and patted the spot beside her. "Come here." Noah scooted next to her. She placed her arm around his shoulders. "Are you okay with me going out tonight?"

"On your date?"

She blinked in surprise. "Yes, my date." She chuckled. "I see I've underestimated you, smart boy."

A pleased smile came over his lips.

"Chas is a good guy," she began.

Noah nodded, waiting for the rest.

Ryleigh bit her lower lip, trying to figure out what to say. "Just because I'm going on a date with Chas doesn't mean that I would ever leave you. I'll only be gone for a few hours, and then I'll be right back."

"I know," he clipped.

She tipped her head. "You do?"

He let out an impatient breath like Ryleigh just didn't get it. "Aunt Tess explained it all to me."

Her head whipped around as she zoned in on Tess's bright red face. Ryleigh's jaw tightened. "What did Aunt Tess say?"

Noah's voice took on the tone of a grown-up. "That Dad was jealous because you're dating a famous football player. That's why he told me you were going to run off with Chas. I know now that it's not true." He looked at Ryleigh with such trust, that it caused tears to well in her eyes. "It's okay to go, Mom. Tess and I'll be fine here."

Tears spilled over Ryleigh's cheeks as she embraced him in a tight hug. "You're something else, sport. I'm so proud of you."

Tess dabbed her eyes, grinning shamefaced at Ryleigh. "You don't give Noah enough credit. He knows how much you love him, and he wants you to be happy. Isn't that right?"

"Yes," Noah answered like he was answering a question in school.

Ryleigh took in a breath as she stood. "All right. I'm off." When she passed Tess, she paused, touching Tess's arm as she whispered. "I know you were trying to help, but in the future, please include me in any heart-to-hearts with Noah, okay?"

"All right," Tess said with a dramatic sigh. She rolled her eyes. "You could just say *thank you*."

Ryleigh softened. "Thank you," she said sincerely, "for everything."

Tess perked right back up. "You're welcome." She flashed a chipper smile. "Have fun, and don't do anything I wouldn't do."

"Well, that opens up a broad spectrum," Ryleigh answered dryly.

Tess let out a light, frothy laugh, then her expression grew serious. "I hope it goes well tonight and that the meeting with Silver Sanchez will help generate some new leads."

Ryleigh caught the flash of worry in Tess's eyes, lurking behind the trivialities, reminding her of the seriousness of their financial situation. "Me too," Ryleigh said, butterflies swarming in her stomach. She was excited about seeing Chas again and nervous about meeting Ace and Silver Sanchez. As she grabbed her car keys from the kitchen table and slipped her purse strap over her shoulder, she offered a silent prayer that all would go well tonight. She glanced at the clock on the microwave before darting out the door. She was running late, but it couldn't be helped. The talk with Noah was more important than being punctual. She smiled thinking of how grownup and practical Noah had sounded. Maybe she hadn't given him enough credit. Tess had spoken to him like an adult, explaining the situation, and Noah had understood.

As she backed out of the carport and pulled onto the road, her heart lurched when she saw a familiar car. She pulled alongside the curb as Joey got out and strode towards her. Her pulse shooting to a higher speed, she rolled down the window.

A large schoolboy smile filled his face. "Wow! You look incredible."

"Thanks," she mumbled. Her brow creased. "Joey, what're you doing here?"

He'd been holding one hand behind his back. He whipped it out, handing her a single red rose. "I wanted to give you this." His voice was soft and intimate as he gazed at her with such a longing expression that it turned her stomach sour.

For a second, she could only look at the rose.

"Take it," he urged.

Robotically, she did so. She didn't bother sniffing it, but placed it on the passenger seat. Then, she clutched the steering wheel with both hands. "Joey, I don't know what you're up to here, but—"

He put a finger to her lips to silence her. The gesture was a violation of her personal space. The hair on her neck bristled as she pushed his finger away with a jerky motion. "I'm late for my date."

She caught a flash of what might've been anger, but before she could be sure of the emotion, Joey masked it with his trademark disarming smile, his even teeth sparkling. There was a time when she would've been dazzled, but not now. Her heart thudded against her chest. "You shouldn't be here. Tess is with Noah. You don't need to go in the house." If Joey tried to go in, it would be disastrous. She wouldn't put it past Tess to call the police, which might not be a bad idea. Joey was starting to freak her out.

"Don't worry. I have no intention of going inside."

She let out a relieved breath. "Good." She frowned. "What're you doing here?" she asked again, not trying to hide the irritation in her voice.

"I wanted to come and see you." He gazed at her like she was the most spectacular thing on the planet. He gave her a significant look, his eyes going a shade darker. She got a good look at him, feeling a little jolted. Tess was right. There was something off about Joey's appearance. The dark circles were still there, his face gaunt. Maybe the stress of being out of work was getting to Joey. She grunted inwardly. That would be a first. She pushed aside the thoughts, focusing on what he was saying. "And tonight, when you're with him, know that I'll be thinking of you." He paused, his jaw working like he was fighting for control of his emotions. "I will always love you."

More unease trickled down her spine like goo that kept oozing out the bottom of a punctured bag. "Joey, that ship sailed a long time ago." There was no other way to confront this except for head-on. Her voice was clipped with a definite edge. "You're doing both of us a disservice by dredging up the past."

Time stood still, both at an impasse.

He cleared his throat, a defiant smile curling his lips as he stepped back and slapped the side of the car with his palm. "Just remember what I said."

She rolled up the window and drove away. When she glanced in her rearview mirror, he was standing in the middle of the road, watching. She got a few blocks away before she glanced at the rose. Looking at it caused her blood to boil with frustration. She rolled down the passenger window, snatched the rose, and tossed it out the window. At the same instant, she felt the jab of pain, realized her finger had been cut on a thorn.

Figures, she muttered, making a mental effort to erase Joey from her brain long enough to enjoy her date.

As RYLEIGH WENT to the door, she used her thumb to put pressure on her index finger to stay the bleeding. The cut wasn't deep, but it wouldn't stop bleeding. The worst was trying to keep blood from getting on her dress. *At least it was red*, so the colors would match. She chuckled inwardly at her poor joke.

The incident with Joey had rattled her more than she cared to admit. The more she pulled away from him, the harder he kept holding on. She'd tried to dance around the topic, but the time for that was past. From now on, she would make it as clear as noonday that she and Joey were over. Not only had the flames from the fire been put out long ago, but even the embers had been thoroughly extinguished.

Chas opened the door. Ryleigh's breath caught as all thoughts of Joey fled. *Wow*. Chas looked even more handsome than normal in his mid-tone blue button-down shirt and khaki slacks. His hair was gelled so that it had a perfect wave to it. One lock fell close to his eye, giving him an adventurous, tumbled look that she rather liked. The color of the shirt picked up the blue in his eyes making them look so striking that it was hard not to stare. Blue magnets sucking her into his wonderful soul, where she could lose herself in utter bliss. His gaze flickered over her. "You look incredible," he murmured, sending heat wafting over her.

She smiled. "Thank you." Suddenly, she was glad she'd worn the red dress. It made her feel feminine and attractive.

He stepped back and motioned. "Come in." Then, he looked down and saw her finger. Concern touched his expression as he tenderly cradled her hands in his. "What happened?"

"I cut myself on the way over."

"How?"

She pushed out a light laugh. "It's not worth going into. Do you have a bandage? The cut's not deep, but it won't stop bleeding."

"Sure, we'll fix you right up." He brought her fingers to his lips and kissed the tips. The gesture sent her cells swirling in a mad dance. He motioned with his head as they went into the kitchen. She glanced at his broad shoulders and how the fabric of his shirt stretched a little across his muscles. He was like a well-oiled machine. Heat pressed against her forehead, and she was flustered at how taken in she was by the masculinity Chas wore like a second skin.

Going straight to the sink, Ryleigh ran cold water over her finger while Chas retrieved a bandage from the cabinet. She glanced around the kitchen and family room. In the warm, golden light of the evening, it felt even more intimate to be here with Chas in his home.

"Here, let me." He blotted her finger with a paper towel and wrapped the bandage around it. Being so close to Chas, having him touch her in such a tender way as though her finger were a priceless object, was doing strange things to her heart.

"Thank you," she said when he'd finished. She soaked in the rugged lines of his face, her eyes tracing the length of his faint scar. It gave him a bad-boy masculine edge that was very tantalizing.

"You really do look incredible," he murmured, his hand stroking her hair. He encircled her waist, pulling her to him. With her red pumps, she was taller than normal, her vision coming to just below his eyes, rather than his chin. She tipped her head back, gazing into his bright blue eyes as a surge of adrenaline rushed through her veins. He was intoxicating, all-consuming, making it difficult to keep a clear head.

"I've missed you," he uttered huskily.

"I've missed you too." He had no idea how much she'd missed him. Every day away from him had felt like torture. She'd occupied herself with work and taking care of Noah. Still, her thoughts had kept returning to Chas, the tide being pulled to the moon.

His eyes longingly traced the outline of her lips. "I'd kiss you right now, but I don't want to smear your lipstick."

The corners of her lips twitched. "You just don't want to get lipstick all over your pretty-boy face," she taunted. He was gorgeous, almost too good looking.

A full smile broke over his lips. "That either. Ace would never let me live it down."

At the mention of Ace's name, the jitters returned full force.

Chas immediately sensed her reservation. "What's wrong?"

"How do you do that?"

"What?"

"Pick up on my feelings."

Light danced in his eyes. "We're connected."

She placed her hands on his chest, noting the hard definition of his muscles. She laughed, some of the anxiety disappearing. "Evidently."

"It's true."

She cocked her head. "All right, Mr. Clairvoyant, what am I thinking right now?"

Amusement flickered in his eyes as he tightened his hold on her waist and began dancing with her. "How after dinner, you'd like to go dancing," he murmured in her ear. "Here, alone, with me."

His warm breath tickled her skin, sending tingles down her spine.

"Is that right?" she managed to say. He smelled good—the combination of soap, mint, and his own distinct masculine scent. His steps were smooth and fluid. "You're a good dancer."

"So are you."

She tipped her head back to look in his eyes. "There's no music."

He wrangled his eyebrows. "I've got the music in my head."

She laughed, feeling lighter than air. Then, her stomach rumbled. She jerked, her eyes widening as heat seeped into her cheeks. "Sorry."

He grinned. "I guess I'm falling short on the mind reading thing. I'm dancing around like a buffoon and all the while you're starving."

"Yeah, I am kind of hungry," she admitted. "I didn't have a chance to eat lunch."

"What?" He gave her an expression of mock astonishment. "The personal chef makes food for everyone else and forgets to feed herself?" He clicked his tongue. "What's the world coming to?"

"Story of my life," she said with a wry grin.

"Well, you're in for a treat tonight. Fabiana's food is legendary." A crooked grin tugged at the corner of his lips. "It might impress even you."

"You make me sound terrible," she protested, making a face.

"No, I didn't mean it like that. You're discriminating."

A chuckle rumbled in her throat. "Ah, is that what I am?"

"You chose me, didn't you?"

"Yes, I did," she laughed. The pleased look in his eyes evoked the same feeling in her. They were choosing each other. She felt like she needed to pinch herself to make sure this was real. She went back to something he'd said. "Who's Fabiana?"

"Ace's mom. She runs the restaurant. Well, both his parents run it, but Fabiana supervises the cooking." He glanced at the clock. "We should probably get going."

"I'm sorry I was a little late."

"No worries. I'm just glad you came." A teasing glint trickled into his eyes. "For a second there, I was afraid you might stand me up."

"No chance of that," she responded confidently, surprising herself again.

"Oh?" he asked lightly, but she caught the gravity in his expression, could sense that everything was weighing on her next comment.

"I'm taking you up on the four-month rule."

He laughed, his beautiful eyes sparkling with delight. "I like the sound of that," he murmured. "Four months will mark the start of the rest of our lives." His eyes caressed hers igniting a slow burn in her stomach. The crazy part was that she was starting to see it—a clear path into their future. They could make this work! "Let's go eat," Chas said. "Then we can come back here to resume our dance ... among other things." His eyes moved to her lips.

A tantalizing shiver trailed like silk down her spine. "Sounds good," she uttered.

"When we get back, remind me to tell you something."

Interest quivered inside her. "What?"

He winked. "It's a surprise."

"Oh?" She wondered what Chas had up his sleeve. "You don't want to tell me now?"

"Nope," he responded lightly. "I wanna save it for the second half."

She laughed. "All right, Irish, we'll save it for the second half." Her stomach rumbled again. She touched it, grimacing.

"Let's get some food in you before your stomach eats your intestines."

"Gross!" She made a face.

"Sorry, that comes from having lots of brothers."

She shook her head. "I'm sure it was fun growing up in your house."

He looked thoughtful. "Yeah, most of the time." He chuckled. "When we weren't killing each other," he said dryly, but she caught the note of affection in his tone. She wondered what Chas's family was like, if his brothers looked like him. There was also the one sister. "It must've been interesting for your sister to grow up with all those brothers."

"I assure you, she can hold her own." He grinned. "She's tougher than the rest of us put together."

"Sounds like Tess."

He pursed his lips. "You know," he mused, "there are some similarities."

They went through the side door into the garage. He went around and opened the passenger door of the Mustang and helped her in.

"Thank you," she said.

When he got seated behind the wheel, she angled to face him. "You're such a gentleman, always opening my door."

He started the engine. "It was the way I was raised, to respect women and children. Even now, my dad would tan my hide if he thought I was doing any different."

Ryleigh smiled. "Kudos to your dad. I hope to instill that in Noah too."

He backed out of the driveway and pulled onto the road. "You will," he said in a sure tone, like there was no possibility of her doing anything else. She appreciated the high level of confidence he had in her.

"You must have good parents." Her heart clutched thinking of her own parents.

"I do," he said. He cast her a sidelong glance, and she caught his curious expression.

"What?"

"Would you like to meet my parents?"

She thought for a minute. "Yeah … sometime. Maybe after the four months," she added.

"Sounds good."

There was something cryptic about his words, making her wonder what was spinning inside his head. Then again, maybe she was reading too much into it. She settled into her seat, getting comfortable. A minute later, he reached for her hand and linked his fingers through hers, sending sparks through her.

One thing was sure, with Chas O'Brien in her life, there was never a dull moment.

12

As they walked into Los Tios, Ryleigh was keenly aware of Chas's hand on the small of her back and how confidently he maneuvered her. Having Chas by her side imbued her with a feeling of enhanced ability and confidence like there was nothing she couldn't accomplish. She marveled at the feeling. Never had she felt this way before, not with Joey nor Dylan. It was exhilarating to be with a man who was an equal partner in the relationship.

The spicy scent of salsa and fresh tortillas filled the air, rumbling her stomach. Festive mariachi music played in the background. The restaurant was crowded, with at least two dozen people crammed in the waiting area.

A pretty, dark-haired girl with almond-shaped eyes and a wide smile greeted them as they approached the hostess counter. "Welcome to Los Tios," she said briskly. "Is it just the two of you?" She glanced down at the paper in front of her. "You're looking at about a twenty to thirty-minute wait. May I get your name?"

Chas cleared his throat. "We're meeting another couple, Ace and Silver Sanchez."

The girl's eyes lit up as her smile grew even larger. "Ace told me to look out for you. Right this way." They followed the girl, meandering through the restaurant to a cozy booth tucked in the back. She smiled brightly, motioning for them to sit. "Have a wonderful dinner."

Ace was sitting on the end. He stood and grabbed Chas's hand, then pulled him in for a hug and hearty pat on the shoulder. "How ya doing, Irish?" he asked in a husky Latino accent.

"Great to see you, man," Chas responded. "This is Ryleigh," he said, motioning to her.

She thrust out her hand. "Hello," she said as they shook.

As Ryleigh scooted into the booth, her gaze swept over Ace and Silver. He was handsome, she was beautiful—a power couple.

Chas sat down and scooted close, draping an arm around her shoulders. Ryleigh turned her attention to Silver. She had long, platinum hair that cascaded in perfect waves over her slender shoulders. Her eyes were crystal blue, a touch lighter than Chas's. She was so poised and put together that she would've been intimidating had her expression not been so warm and open. "Hi," Ryleigh began, extending her hand. "It's nice to meet you."

"Likewise," Silver smiled.

"How goes it with the Titans?" Ace asked. "Are you enjoying your downtime?"

"Every minute."

"You had one heck of a season, man." Ace rattled off a few of the same stats Tess had read online.

"Thanks," Chas responded with a casual flick of his hand. "Just trying to fill your shoes."

A smile pulled at Ace's lips. "I think you're doing just fine." Ace sat back in his seat. "So, word on the street is that you're one of the lucky bachelors at the annual Titan's auction." His mouth quirked with humor. "When is it?"

"The weekend before Valentine's Day," Chas said flatly.

Auction? Bachelor? Ryleigh's spine stiffened as she gave Chas a questioning look. The pinched look on his face let her know that the answer wasn't going to be pleasant.

"I have to participate in a charity auction. A few of the Titan players are being auctioned off for dates to the highest bidders." The note of disgust in Chas's voice was loud and clear. "Players are asked to participate with the clear expectation that we'll say *yes*."

Silver jutted her thumb at Ace. "He had to do it too."

Ace cringed. "I hated every minute of it." He shuddered. "I'm glad I don't have to go through that dog and pony show again." He flashed a bright smile at Chas. "Well, good luck to ya, amigo."

Ryleigh felt Chas watching her. "What?" she asked quietly, trying to downplay her irritation. She didn't want women bidding on Chas like he was a piece of meat. The thoughts of it made her stomach churn. She was surprised at how unnerved she was by this news.

"It's no big deal." Chas's eyes held hers. "When I agreed to do it, I was unattached."

"Aw, you'll survive. Just grin and bear it like the rest of us did." Ace winked at Ryleigh. "You can even take your lady with you, if you want. I did."

For a split second, Ryleigh wondered if she'd heard him correctly. "Really?" That seemed weird.

"Yep," Ace clipped, grinning like a Cheshire Cat.

"I was the event planner in charge of the date," Silver clarified, rolling her eyes at Ace.

Chas chuckled in surprise. "You planned the date?"

"Uh, huh," Silver said.

"That's even worse," Chas lamented.

A smile played on Silver's lips. "Yes, it was." Her eyes lit with mischief. "Of course, the woman Ace was having dinner with got furious because he was paying more attention to me than her."

"True story," Ace hooted. "All night long, I couldn't take my eyes off her." He gave Silver a treasured look. "Not much has changed."

"So," Chas asked, his eyes stirring with amusement, "would you like to plan my bachelor auction date?"

"Not on your life," Ryleigh barked as everyone laughed. Her cheeks were blistered from heat, and she felt like a fist was jabbed into her stomach. While everyone else found the auction amusing, she certainly didn't.

Silver caught Ryleigh's eye and grinned like the two of them were old friends. "I don't think you need to worry about Chas. It's obvious that he only has eyes for you."

An unexpected wave of warmth rolled over Ryleigh, diffusing the situation.

"Amen to that," Chas boomed.

"How does the team look for next season?" Ace asked, resting his arm on the back of the booth.

Chas answered with a long, detailed explanation of the players and what the coaches were having them do to get ready.

Finally, after a good ten minutes of back and forth conversation between Chas and Ace, Silver caught Ryleigh's eye. "They'll go on like this all night, if we let them. Meanwhile, you and I'll poke our eyeballs out with a dull fork."

A surprised laugh gurgled in Ryleigh's throat.

"You know you love it." Ace slid his arm around her shoulder, planting a kiss on her cheek.

Silver laughed, her eyes softening as she gave him an adoring look. "Football not so much, but I love you."

"I can live with that," Ace said, a giant grin on his face like he'd won the jackpot.

It was touching to see the deep affection between Ace and Silver.

"You sound like Ryleigh," Chas said, tightening his arm around her. He rumbled out a low chuckle. "She didn't even know my last name, much less which position I play."

Silver flashed Ryleigh an appraising look. "Sounds like the two of us are kindred spirits."

At that one statement, all of Ryleigh's reservations about the evening vanished. "Yes," she agreed with a laugh.

A female server in her early thirties approached with a platter of chips and salsa.

"About time," Ace said with a teasing smile.

The woman harrumphed. "It's not for you, but your better half." She placed the basket of chips on the table, along with two bowls of salsa.

"Thank you, Carmen," Silver chimed in a singsong voice.

"I don't know how you put up with him," Carmen countered, but there was a note of affection in her voice.

"Carmen's my cousin," Ace explained.

Carmen's eyes widened as she put a finger to her lips, glancing over her shoulder. "Shh, don't say that out loud. I don't want people to know I'm related to you."

Ace winced, his dark eyes radiating laughter. He flicked his wrist like his fingers had been burned. "Ouch! See what I have to put up with?"

"You give as much as you take," Carmen grumbled, then slipped back into her business persona. "All right. What can I get you to drink?"

After Carmen took the drink orders, she perched a hand on her hip. "Are you ready to order, or do you need a minute to look at the menus?"

It was then that Ryleigh realized she hadn't even opened her menu. Chas seemed to be reading her mind. "If we could have another few minutes, that would be great," he said politely.

Carmen looked at Chas, then looked again, eyes bulging as she pointed. "I know you. You're the Irish Flash," she said, her voice rising. A giddy laugh skittered in her throat. "My sons won't believe it when I tell them that I met you. I've gotta find something in the kitchen for you to autograph."

Ace grunted. "Titan players come in here all the time, Carmen. I've never seen you get googly eyed before." He reached for a chip, scooped out a large amount of salsa, and placed it in his mouth.

"Well, not all of them are the Irish Flash," Carmen countered, lifting her chin. "This guy's fast," she said, awe tinging her voice.

"Thanks," Chas said offhandedly, color seeping into his face.

It was cute how uncomfortable Chas was under the praise. Ace noticed it too. "All right, Carmen, let the man enjoy his dinner. After our meal, you can get your autograph."

"You're just jealous because I'm not fawning over you," Carmen said tartly.

Ace chuckled. "Yeah, that's it."

Carmen snorted. "What is this anyway, the Titan's running back club?" She looked at Chas. "I guess that makes you member number three."

Ryleigh had no idea what Carmen was talking about, and it must've shown on her face because Silver piped in. "She's referring to Rennen Bradley, the running back who replaced Ace on the Titans team. Then, Chas took Rennen's spot. So, it's one, two, and three. Rennen is married to Ace's sister Ariana."

"Really?" Ryleigh's jaw went slack. "What a small world. That must've been interesting."

Silver chuckled, her light eyes raining laughter. "Oh, it was. From the minute Rennen joined the family, the competition between him and Ace has never stopped."

"I still hold the title for eating the most tamales," Ace said with a touch of pride, as everyone laughed.

Carmen gave Chas the once over like she was inspecting a dessert she was about to dig into. "You are a cutie," she quipped as she turned on her heel and sauntered away.

Ryleigh realized that Silver was studying her with perceptive eyes that saw right through her. Ryleigh guessed Silver could tell she had a hard time with women fawning over Chas every second. "You'll get used to all the fanfare."

"Will I?" Ryleigh asked. She shook her head. "I dunno. The other day in the grocery store, I thought I was going to have to fight off a couple women," she said dryly.

"Yep, I remember those days," Silver said.

"Hey," Ace said, making a long face. "You don't think I'm all that anymore?"

"You'll always be all that to me," Silver assured him, placing a hand over his. "Every dog has its day. Now it's Chas's turn." She winked at Ryleigh and Chas before continuing. "I think it's safe to say that the only football you'll be playing is with our kids when they get old enough."

Ryleigh's stomach rumbled. She clutched it, hoping no one had heard. She reached for a chip and dipped it into the salsa. The tangy chipotle flavor burst in her mouth, blending perfectly with the light, flaky chip. It was really good. No wonder the restaurant was packed. Chas dug into the chips and salsa also. A comfortable silence ensued as everyone began eating.

"How many children do you have?" Ryleigh asked a couple minutes later.

"One daughter who's beautiful like her mom and two sons," Ace answered. He looked at Chas. "Silver's right. My plate's full. I gladly abdicate the throne to you, man," he joked.

Ryleigh could tell that for all his talk, it didn't bother Ace in the slightest that Chas was in the spotlight instead of him. Ace seemed comfortable with himself and his life. In fact, both he and Silver seemed happy. That's what she wanted, a partner to share her life with.

Chas turned to her, a pained look on his handsome face. "I'm sorry," he winced. "I know it's a pain to go out with me in public, but like Silver said, it'll pass. At the end of the day, you'll be left with just plain, old me." He gave her a searching look, and she caught the tinge of vulnerability in his sapphire eyes. It struck a chord inside her. For an instant, everyone and everything but Chas vanished.

"That's good," she said sagely, "because you're all that I want. The rest of it is just fluff." Had she really just said that out loud? Yes, she had. It was official. She wanted him and not just for four months. She wanted him for good.

He rewarded her with a brilliant smile. She remembered then that they weren't alone. She cleared her throat, glancing at Silver and Ace as a couple of awkward seconds passed.

"I think the two of you are going to be just fine," Silver said, her eyes holding the knowledge of one who'd fought her own battles and come out the victor. She focused her full attention on Ryleigh. "What do you do professionally?"

It was the moment of truth. Ryleigh sensed that Chas was bursting at the seams for her to tell Silver all about herself. "I'm a personal chef."

"Wow, that's awesome," Silver said, her expression one of genuine interest.

"Yes, it is," Ace agreed. "You and Silver run in similar circles. As I mentioned earlier, she used to be an event planner. Now, she and I spend the bulk of our time overseeing our restaurants."

"That's fantastic," Ryleigh said.

"Ryleigh's an amazing chef. She's participating in the Grilling and Chilling Cooking Competition coming up in the next few weeks," Chas said, his chest swelling with pride.

Silver's eyes rounded. "You must be really good."

"Thank you." Now it was Ryleigh's turn to be uncomfortable with the praise. "I'm trying to expand my business, get the word out."

Ace grew thoughtful as he turned to Silver. "You know lots of people in that arena."

"Yes, I do. Do you have any cards? I'll be happy to spread the word," Silver said.

It was all Ryleigh could do to keep a straight face. "That would be fantastic. Thank you." She reached in her purse and pulled out a handful of cards, handing them to Silver who read over the information before placing the cards in her purse. Ace and Silver were good, down-to-earth people. Ace's fame hadn't tarnished them one iota. Seeing them together was very encouraging.

Carmen returned with the drinks. She passed them out, then pulled a pad out of her apron. She wet the tip of her finger with her tongue, then flipped a page, her pen poised to write. "All right," she sighed. "What would you like to eat?"

Laughter rang out around the table.

"What?" Carmen asked dubiously.

"We've been so busy talking, we haven't had a chance to look at the menu," Chas explained apologetically.

Carmen wagged a finger. "Now, Irish, do I have to tell you how this works? At this rate y'all will be here all night, which is fine with me because I've got plenty of time, but I figure your pretty lady might be getting antsy."

Ryleigh smiled, nodding slightly at Carmen to acknowledge her compliment. At least Carmen had the good grace to recognize that Chas was here with a date.

"What're y'all getting?" Chas asked Ace and Silver.

Ace drummed his fingers on the table. "I'll have the enchilada combination platter."

"I want the chicken chimichanga platter," Silver said.

Chas opened the menu and glanced at the items. "I'll take one of each," he joked. He turned to Ryleigh. "What're you getting?"

She opened the menu, not really needing to look at it to know what she wanted. "I think I'll try the chicken and shrimp fajitas."

"Good choice," Silver said. "I almost got those, but I just had them recently."

"As you can imagine, Silver and I get our fair share of Mexican food," Ace laughed.

Carmen's eyebrow shot up, letting him know at once that he'd said the wrong thing.

Ace held up a hand. "Not that I'm complaining. We love it." He leaned forward and whispered. "Just not every single meal."

Carmen swiped him across the head.

"Ouch!" he complained ducking out of her reach.

"That's for your mama," Carmen said vindication sounding in her voice. "She'd do the same if she heard you."

"Yes, she would," Ace acknowledged with an indulgent grin. "Please don't tell her."

"I've got my eye on you," Carmen warned. Then, she turned to Chas, her voice going syrupy sweet. "All right, honey. What'll you have?"

Ryleigh looked at Silver, whose eyes were bubbling with laughter. She, too, had noticed how quickly Carmen turned on the charm for Chas. A smile twitched at Ryleigh's lips as she looked down to suppress her laughter. Silver was the type of person she could be good friends with.

"Make Ryleigh's fajitas a double, and we'll share," Chas said. "Oh, and can you bring some extra guacamole?"

"Sure thing, sugar." Carmen winked. "All right. I'll get these orders put in for ya."

Silver's phone rang. "Excuse me," she said as she dug it out of her pocket. "It's my daughter Gracie, I need to take this. She and the boys are with a babysitter tonight. Hi, honey," she said into the phone. "Is everything okay?"

Ace's demeanor changed immediately as his attention shifted to Silver and the conversation.

Apprehension carved over Silver's features. "Did Riley say how long you would be gone?"

Ryleigh jumped slightly at the mention of her name, then realized Silver was referring to someone else.

"Who else is going … I'm not saying you can't go, Gracie. Ace and I need to discuss it. Also, I need to talk to Riley and get more details." Her voice rose. "No, I don't want Riley to call me right now." Her eyes flickered to Ryleigh and Chas as she flashed an apologetic smile. "Honey, now's not a good time for this conversation." Ace placed a reassuring hand on Silver's arm. She gave him a brief smile as if to say she had everything under control, but she looked strained. "It's not that I don't want to talk about it, but Ace and I are in the middle of dinner. Gracie, let's talk about this later tonight when I get home. How are things going with the babysitter? Are the boys minding?"

"Tell them they'd better," Ace added in an authoritative tone.

Silver nodded, acknowledging his comment. "All right. We'll talk soon. I love you. Bye." She ended the call, shaking her head.

Ace frowned. "What was that all about?"

"Riley—" she stopped and looked at Ryleigh as if realizing that she had the same name as the person she'd been referring to. "Riley's my ex-husband and Gracie's father."

Ryleigh felt as though she and Chas were intruding on a private matter. She glanced at Chas, who seemed to be reading her thoughts, then back to Silver. "If y'all need to leave early, we understand."

"Absolutely," Chas agreed.

Ace looked at Silver. "Do we need to leave? What's going on?"

She placed her phone back into her purse with a heavy sigh. "No, the babysitter and kids are fine."

"What's going on?" Ace prompted.

"Riley called. He wants to take Gracie to Disney World next week."

His brows furrowed. "What?" he fumed. "In the middle of the school term?" Ace asked with an incredulous tone. "Unbelievable!" he muttered. "Why's he just now bringing this up? You don't plan a trip like that on the spur of the moment."

Silver spread her hands. "Who knows? Probably to make things difficult. You know how Riley is."

"Who else is going?" Ace demanded.

"Riley's parents, his girlfriend, and her two kids."

Ace's jaw clenched. "I don't think it's a good idea for Gracie to go all the way to Florida with those people."

Silver gave Ace an indulgent smile. "I know how protective you are of Gracie."

"Dang straight, I am," Ace said, his jaw tight.

"I told Gracie we'd discuss it when you and I get home." Silver's voice was controlled like she was trying to keep the peace. She looked at Ryleigh and Chas. "I'm so sorry." She huffed out a humorless laugh. "You're getting more than you bargained for this evening."

"Yes, you are," Ace agreed. He looked at Chas. "Sorry, man. You're getting an inside look at a day in the life of the Sanchezes, I'm afraid."

Chas waved a hand. "No worries."

"My ex-husband's hard to deal with," Silver added.

"That's an understatement." Ace scowled. "The guy's an idiot. He doesn't give a hoot about Gracie. He just likes using her as a bargaining chip to spite me and Silver."

"You're more of a father to Gracie than Riley will ever be," Silver said. "One day, when Gracie becomes an adult, she'll realize that. Gracie has Down Syndrome," Silver explained. "She's smart as a whip but her development is a little behind."

"But when she gets it, she gets it," Ace said.

Silver nodded. "Very true."

Ace let out a long breath. "Riley's just trying to push our buttons."

"Yep, that's exactly what he's doing." Her eyes narrowed. "And, every time he does, Gracie gets caught in the middle."

Like Noah just did. The similarity was too much. Ryleigh couldn't hold back the laugh tickling her throat. When it came out, everyone looked at her in surprise. She held up a hand. "I'm sorry, I mean no disrespect. It's just that I can totally relate to everything you're going through. My ex-husband has been giving me grief all week. In fact, that's why I was running late." She looked at Chas who wore an expression of surprise. "My ex had the audacity to show up at my house as I was leaving to give me a rose." She held up her bandaged finger, a sardonic chuckle escaping her lips. "In a fit of anger, I threw it out the window and cut my finger." She couldn't believe that she'd just spilled her guts to Chas and his friends. Admittedly, it felt good to get it off her chest, but still … some things were better left unsaid.

Chas turned towards her. "Why didn't you tell me?"

She shrugged. "I don't know. I guess I didn't want to ruin our evening."

"Ex's," Silver grumbled.

"Amen," Ryleigh quipped with a laugh.

"Do you have any kids with your ex?" Silver asked.

Ryleigh nodded. "Yes, a seven-year-old son, Noah. He's in the second grade."

Silver gave her a wise look. "I know we've just met, and I have no idea what kind of man your ex-husband is, but if I could give you any advice it would be not to let whatever happened in the past ruin your present and future." Silent information passed between Silver and Ace as they looked at each other. "I lost a lot of good years down that road." Regret simmered in Silver's eyes as she bit her lower lip.

"It all worked out well in the end, babe," Ace said tenderly. "We got Gracie, each other, and our boys."

"Yes, we did," Silver said, giving him a radiant smile.

A pang went through Ryleigh's heart. Silver couldn't know it, but she'd hit the nail on the head. Ryleigh had to move forward with her life and embrace the wonderful opportunities she'd been given, Chas being at the top of the list. Moisture rose in Ryleigh's eyes. She swallowed, trying to hold it back. She couldn't lose it now! Chas looked at her, realized she was struggling. He offered a smile and began rubbing circles on her shoulders. She looked down, swallowing to stay the emotion.

Luckily, the food arrived a second later, giving Ryleigh the welcome distraction she needed to pull herself together. "Um, that looks good," Chas said as Carmen placed the cast iron skillet of sizzling fajitas in front of them.

"Yes, it does," Ryleigh agreed, the savory scent enveloping her senses.

Chas surprised her by reaching for her hand under the table and squeezing it tightly. His eyes latched onto hers for one quick second, but it was enough to give her all the reassurance she needed to know that she was making the right decision about him. She'd also lost a lot of good years on the wrong road. Time to get on the right one and stay on it!

13

When Ace mentioned the Bachelor Auction over dinner, Chas had wanted to crawl under the table, especially when he saw Ryleigh's startled expression. When the Titan execs approached him about doing the auction, he'd not been too worried about it. He and Selena's relationship was on the rocks, and Chas knew it would only be a matter of time before he was unattached. What he hadn't counted on, however, was meeting Ryleigh. Now, he wanted to just get the stupid thing over with. Thankfully, it wasn't taking place for a couple more weeks. The downside was that he was supposed to go on a date with the winner on Valentine's Day. Chas dreaded breaking the news to Ryleigh.

Ryleigh's announcement about her ex-husband giving her the rose came at Chas like a refrigerator-sized lineman from behind. Was her ex still in the picture? He thought back to the conversation he and Ryleigh had where she said that she'd been divorced four years and that she and her ex were friends. His gut twisted. From the sound of things her ex wanted more. In the sports world, the key to winning the game was knowing the strengths and weaknesses of your competition. Chas realized with a jolt that he knew very little about Ryleigh's ex.

He pulled his eyes off the road for a moment as he glanced at Ryleigh's delicate profile. She'd been quiet since they left the restaurant. "Is everything okay? You're awfully quiet."

"So are you," she countered in a soft, playful tone.

"I suppose you're right," he chuckled.

"What're you thinking?"

"How wonderful you were tonight." He reached for her hand. "Ace and Silver loved you."

"Thank you, but I think you're a little biased."

He caught the smile in her voice. "I can't argue with you there."

"I like Ace and Silver too ... a lot." She paused. "Can I ask you a question?"

"Sure," he said lightly, but he could tell the wheels were spinning in her head. He didn't know if that was a good or bad thing.

"Why did you want me to meet Silver and Ace?"

Not what he was expecting. He thought she would bring up the Bachelor Auction. "Well, for starters, I thought Silver would be a good contact for your business."

"Yes," she said quickly, "I think she will be. Thank you so much for talking me up the way you did."

"Everything I said was true. You're an amazing chef." He hoped she realized how sincere he was.

"Thank you." A few seconds passed. "Was there any other reason you wanted me to meet them?"

He thought for a minute. "Well, Ace is one of my closest friends, and I'd hoped that you'd get along with Silver. It would be nice to get together with them occasionally." He cast her a sidelong glance. She had a pensive expression, and he could tell she was working her way up to something. "What is it you want to ask?"

"Did you know about Silver's ex-husband and how similar our situations are?" she blurted. "Were you hoping that by seeing how well Ace and Silver get along that I would feel like there's hope for us?"

He flinched at the forthrightness of her questions. "I knew that

Silver had been married before, and that she had a daughter from that marriage."

"I see."

The accusation in her voice caught him off guard. It stung. "No, I didn't realize that Silver and Ace don't get along with her ex. Nor did I realize that you don't get along with yours. You told me that you and your ex were friends."

"Oh," she stammered. "I haven't told you the latest." Her tone was apologetic, conciliatory.

"Nope," he answered curtly, "you haven't." He released her hand. "So, if you're asking if tonight was a setup, then the answer is a resounding *no*."

A tense silence froze between them as Chas concentrated on the dark road, illuminated by the headlights.

"I'm sorry," Ryleigh finally said. "I had no right to insinuate that you were trying to pull a fast one." She let out a shaky laugh. "It's just that my situation with my ex-husband is so similar to what Silver described, I couldn't help but think …" Her voice trailed off. "I shouldn't have jumped to conclusions." She touched his arm. "Forgive me, please?"

That's all it took for the anger to completely vanish. "Of course," he said, flashing a reassuring smile. "I would like to hear the full story," he prompted. The darkness of the night settled around them like a protective blanket, making Chas feel as though he and Ryleigh were the only two people in the world. He realized with a jolt that it wouldn't take much for her to make up his entire world. Well, except for his family to whom he was very close. He'd never met a woman who he felt could be everything to him. Ryleigh was fast becoming that, which is why he needed to know the situation with her ex-husband.

Ryleigh took in an audible breath. "All right. Here's the short of it. The day I made the food for you, Tess took care of Noah."

"Yes."

"Well, when I got home that evening, Noah was still awake."

Tension crackled in her voice. "He asked me if I was going to run away with the football player I was dating."

Chas tightened his grip on the steering wheel. "What? Where did he get that idea?"

"Joey had stopped by," she spat, "and filled Noah's head with nonsense."

Anger flared over Chas like a blow torch. He wanted to punch Joey in the face and he'd never even met him. Apprehension twisted in Chas's gut. "Did you tell Noah that was not the case."

"Oh, absolutely. The next day, I let Joey have it." Her voice grew brittle. "On the surface, what Joey did sounds bad, but when you know my history, it's deplorable. My mother left when I was ten." Her voice shook. "Joey knows how hard that was for me and Tess. My dad basically shut down, leaving me and Tess to fend for ourselves."

A pang of compassion shot through Chas. He wanted to scoop Ryleigh into his arms and erase the hurt. "I'm sorry," he said lamely. Those two words seemed so inadequate, but he didn't know what else to say.

"My dad's not a bad person. When I was a kid, I hated him for the empty look in his eyes." She balled her fist. "I just wanted him to feel something ... anything!"

Silence lapsed between them.

Ryleigh grew practical. "Now that I'm older, I realize that he was getting through it the best he could." The words came out dispassionate like she was reading from a script, maybe hoping that if she repeated it often enough, she'd start to believe it. "My dad got remarried to Carol who helped him fill the hole in his heart." She grew hoarse. "Tess and I hoped that with Carol in his life Dad would return to us." She cleared her throat. "Unfortunately, that wasn't the case. Carol succeeded in driving a wedge between us that exists to this day. But that no longer matters." Her voice cracked. "What matters is that I have Noah to look after. Above all, I want Noah to know that I'll never leave him ... not for anyone or anything."

He didn't have to look at Ryleigh to know she was crying. He pulled into his driveway and hit the remote on the sun visor. When they were inside the garage, he turned off the engine and closed the door. Even though it was dark, Chas felt like he was truly seeing Ryleigh for the first time. "I can't imagine what you've been through." He angled towards her, a chilling thought occurring to him. "Every person in your life, with the exception of Tess and Noah, has let you down."

Ryleigh wiped her eyes, half-laughing, still half-crying. "Pretty much. It's pitiful, isn't it?"

What kind of man—monster—would use his own seven-year-old son to manipulate the child's mother? He'd met plenty of Joey's type in his line of work—the type that had no scruples, the kind willing to stoop to any level to win.

Chas wanted to win as much as the next guy. No, he wanted it more than most, which is what made him successful. However, there were lines you didn't cross. His parents had taught him that character was more important than the win. Much of his identity had been shaped by his parents' influence. Chas was brought up with the knowledge that there was no goal, within reason, he couldn't obtain if he was willing to work hard enough. What must it have been like for Ryleigh, having to scratch and claw her way up with no help? Also, she was responsible for her younger sister. No wonder Ryleigh struggled with confidence. She was a remarkable woman accomplishing all that she had, notwithstanding her circumstances.

He touched her cheek, rubbing her tears away with his thumb. His next words came from somewhere deep inside his core. "I won't let you down." Never had a statement hit him more forcibly than this one did here and now.

She didn't speak right away, but sniffed instead. Then, a weak smile touched her lips. It was barely visible in the dim light of the garage. "You know what? I believe you."

A swell of victory ran through him. No, not victory but a feeling of completeness like he'd finally found the one he'd searched for his entire life. He jumped slightly, not expecting this revelation to come so soon in the relationship. Nevertheless, here it was. Tenderness welled inside him as he leaned close and planted a soft kiss on her lips, then he rested his head against her forehead. "I'm falling hard for you, Ryleigh Eisenhart."

"Ditto," she responded.

Excitement trickled through his veins. "Let's go inside, and I'll tell you the surprise."

She laughed. "Oh, yeah. I forgot about that." She reached for the door handle.

"Don't touch that," he ordered. "My daddy would tan my hide," he sang in a cavalier drawl.

"We can't be having that, now can we?" she said, playfully mimicking his tone.

An amused smile twitched at his lips. "No, we most certainly can't." Her spirits were lifting. That was good. Hopefully, Ryleigh would be happy about what he was about to tell her.

A DEEP EXHAUSTION seeped into Ryleigh's bones as she stepped into Chas's kitchen. She cringed inwardly when he flipped on the lights. She was sure she looked awful, all red-eyed and puffy faced.

Chas deposited his keys on the island. "Let's go sit down on the couch." His countenance glowed with anticipation. Ryleigh couldn't imagine what the surprise was. As they sat down on the deep chocolate leather couch, Ryleigh instinctively rubbed her hand over the expensive, soft leather. An image of her worn, thread-bare couch flitted through her mind. She and Tess had put a slipcover over it to give a few more years' use.

"What're you thinking about?"

"Huh?" A contrite smile pushed over her lips. "I was just thinking how nice your couch is." Her cheeks warmed a little.

He laughed in surprise, the sound coming out rich and full like a demi-glace sauce.

Her hand went up to tuck hair behind her ear. "I'm a wreck." She felt vulnerable and embarrassed that she'd told Chas all those things about her past. He probably thought she was giving him a sob story so he'd feel sorry for her. Her stomach twisted. She didn't want this relationship to be built on pity. She sat up straight, wetting her lips, needing to explain why she'd told him all that she had. "When Silver told us about her past ..." she shifted "... when I saw the depth of love that Ace has for Silver's daughter, a child that's not his." Her jaw worked. "Well, it hit me hard." A short laugh escaped her lips as she clasped her hands together tightly in her lap. Chas placed a hand over hers. The warmth of his skin was so comforting it was almost hypnotic. She was embarrassed to be speaking so openly, yet she needed to get it out. "It gave me a glimpse of what we could have together someday."

Chas rewarded her with a radiant smile. "Yes," he exclaimed jubilantly.

She frowned. "Then, on the way home, I started second guessing everything. The evening was so perfect that it felt like a setup." His handsome face drained. "That's why I asked you how much you knew about Ace and Silver's past. Don't worry, I realize that I was over-analyzing, something I do quite often." She chuckled darkly. "Tess always tells me that I have a knack for finding the one cloud with a dark underlining in a sky full of white, puffy clouds." Tears glistened in her eyes as she flashed a regretful smile. "I don't mean to be that way, but it's something I have to fight against."

He cupped both hands around hers. His arresting face was one of contemplation as he tipped his head. "As you can imagine, in my field there's much focus on motor skill learning. How a player runs or catches the ball is vital. The right movements can lead to measurable success, the wrong to injuries or failure. The athlete's movements are assessed and the weakness pinpointed. Then the retraining begins. Generally, there's a fast phase and slow phase of learning. The fast phase involves an intense training session where you make yourself repeat the correct motion over and over." He chuckled ruefully. "It's painful. At the end of this session, your brain knows the correct movement, but it's still foreign to your body. That's where the slow phase comes in. You make slow, steady improvements over a long period of time until, eventually, your brain and body movements sync. Then, you reach your optimum performance level."

"Where you can achieve measurable success," she added, the corners of her lips twitching.

"Yes." A crooked grin slid over his mouth. "Sorry for all the football analogies. It's the easiest way for me to explain my thoughts."

She mulled over his comments. They made sense. "So, what you're saying is that tonight I had a fast phase learning session."

He chuckled. "Yes, that's exactly what I'm saying."

She pursed her lips, reaching a decision. "All right, I'll go with that." She drank in his chiseled features, the confident set of his lean jaw, the wise light in his beautiful eyes. "Let the second learning phase begin," she said glibly, but the truth of Chas's words found a place in her heart. She would work on her thought processes.

The tips of his fingers trailed sensuously over the curve of her jaw. "We'll take it slow and easy."

Heat simmered in her stomach. "Yes," she whispered, leaning in for a kiss.

He pulled her into his arms. His warm lips were as delicate as a feather-light meringue as they brushed coaxingly on hers. She savored his delicious taste as her hands slipped around his neck. The aching need for him grew as she rubbed her hands over the ridges of his sinewy back muscles, committing every facet of him to memory. When his strong arms encircled her waist, her body trembled as a fiery blaze ignited between them giving an avenue for her weary heart to melt into. She clung to him, reveling in every divine sensation he evoked.

He pulled back, assessing her face. The tenderness in his eyes nearly caused her to turn to a puddle of mush. Ever so lightly, he traced her lips. "You are the most incredible woman I've ever met."

"You're not so bad yourself, Irish," she quipped.

His eyes brightened with pleasure. "How do you do that?"

"What?"

He chuckled under his breath. "Make my tired old nickname sound so sexy."

"You are sexy," she said shyly, a small smile quivering over her lips. "The sexiest man I've ever met."

He gave her a slow, leisurely smile that sent her pulse racing. "I could say the same about you."

She touched his hair. "It's so thick," she mused.

He quirked a frown. "It's a mop."

A ripple of mirth bubbled in her chest. "And what a lovely carrot-top mop it is." She couldn't wait any longer. "All right, what's your surprise?"

He took in a breath, and she could sense an undercurrent of something—apprehension, excitement—running beneath his placid expression. "My mother's fifty-ninth birthday is next Saturday."

"Oh?" Her mind jumped ahead, trying to figure out where this was going.

He clasped her hands, squeezing them. "My dad has been planning a party with family and a few close friends."

Her throat tightened. "Are you going to New Orleans next weekend?" She was taken aback by how unnerved she was at the thought of him leaving.

"Yes."

The question flew out of her mouth. "How long will you be gone?" She hated the desperate edge in her voice. *Sheesh*. It was crazy and a little scary how quickly she'd become invested in Chas.

"Just for the weekend."

"Oh." A relieved smile spilled over her lips. She got a good look at him and realized he was jittery. "What else? What's the surprise?"

"Well, I spoke to my dad today. He'd had a caterer lined up for a couple months, but it fell through." He gave her a searching look. "I was hoping you could fill the slot."

Her heart began to pound. "Me?" she squeaked.

His words rushed out. "I realize it's last minute."

"How many guests?"

He tipped his head. "I'm guessing around twenty, but I can get you an exact number."

"How long would we be gone?"

"We would leave on Thursday evening and come back Sunday. I realize that this would be a lot of work for you, especially considering it's last minute."

"In a location I'm unfamiliar with," she said, thinking out loud. She bit her lower lip. "I'd have to do some research on suppliers."

"Of course," he said smoothly. "I'll be glad to help any way I can." He cleared his throat. "Not to make this awkward, but my dad had negotiated a price of $5K with the caterer."

She thought for a minute. "Is it a formal dinner?"

"I think so."

That was a good price. Well, it would be here in Ft. Worth or Dallas, if Ryleigh had access to her suppliers.

"I'll pay you an extra ten thousand on top of that. It's the least I can do for the extra time and trouble."

Ryleigh's jaw dropped. "What?" Her head spun like a hamster ball with her scrambled brain running endless circles. The money was so tempting, especially in her current circumstance. Man, oh, man was it tempting! All she had to say was *yes*, and her money issues would be solved ... at least for a few months. She could get caught up on bills, buy some new cooking tools, tuck some money aside for a rainy day. It was all she could do to push the words out, a gloom spreading through her stomach. "No, that's too much. We're involved. It wouldn't be right to take your money." She couldn't let Chas throw money at her. She had to remain principled.

"I want to give it to you." His expression was imploring as he searched her eyes. "Please, let me help you."

She flinched, understanding registering. Her lips formed a rigid battle line, eyes narrowing. "Help me?"

His face fell. "Yes, is that so bad?"

"How do you know that I need help?" She gave him a hard look. "Has Gemma been running her mouth about my business?" Her best client or not, if Gemma were here, Ryleigh would give her a piece of her mind.

He rubbed his neck. "Yeah, she might've mentioned something about you needing more clients."

Her hand went to her forehead as she laughed humorlessly. "Gemma needs to learn to keep her big mouth shut. I'm doing just fine," she said, lifting her chin.

"Look, this isn't just about your business. My dad is at his wits' end. He wants the party to be special for my mom. I need your help." His eyes pled with hers. "Will you help me? Say, *yes*," he urged.

He was so dang cute with his puppy-dog eyes that she couldn't help but soften. Her mind ticked through the details. "I'll have to talk to Tess and see if she can keep Noah."

Chas didn't skip a beat. "He can come too."

She chuckled dryly. "No, I wouldn't be able to get any work done. Noah's high energy with a short attention span."

"I can look after him."

She touched Chas's jaw, an unconscious laugh leaving her throat. "You'd do that for me?"

"Of course."

"You're so good to me. Thank you." Her eyes grew moist. "I'm grateful that you came into my life."

"Me too."

She laughed. "You're grateful that you came into my life, too?" she teased. "I know, I need all the help I can get."

"We all need help of one form or fashion."

The truth of his words hit home. "Yes, you're right."

A smile tugged at his lips. "And, yes, I'm grateful that you came into my life." His eyes were two big, sparkling seas of untapped adventures. "So, will you come to New Orleans with me?"

Excitement trickled through her. "As long as I can get Tess lined up to watch Noah, then yes, I will." She paused, giving him a steely look. "But I won't let you to pay me some ridiculous amount. I'm sure the amount your dad negotiated with the other caterer will be sufficient." Even if Ryleigh could clear half the amount for a weekend's work, it would be well worth it … assuming Chas covered her plane fare and accommodations. She was sure he would, without question.

"We'll see," he said evasively.

She arched an eyebrow. "No, you won't see." She shoved his arm.

A smile played on his lips as he caught hold of her wrist. "You're a stubborn little thing, aren't you?"

"You have no idea," she replied, squaring her jaw.

He caught hold of her other wrist, holding them both in a tight grip as his eyes lit with a wicked glint. "Now, for the most important question." He leaned in, the motion pushing her back onto the couch as he wrangled his eyebrows.

He was so devastatingly handsome that it nearly took her breath away. "What?" she laughed, itching to kiss him again.

"Are you ticklish?"

Her eyes bugged. "You wouldn't!"

"Oh, yes, I would," he countered, tickling her mercilessly.

14

Ever since Ryleigh had agreed to go with Chas to New Orleans, he'd been on top of the world. It had been a busy week for Ryleigh as she took care of her clients while doing as much preparation for the dinner party as she could remotely. Chas acted as liaison between Ryleigh and his dad. The good news was that his dad wasn't particular about the details. Dad's only requirement was that there be an even mix of beef and chicken on the menu so the guests could choose. Ryleigh spent an entire day online and making phone calls to scout out the best wholesale suppliers to use, both for the food and party rental equipment. After narrowing it down to two, she emailed them her tax ID number and other pertinent information to set up the accounts. The plan was for them to purchase as much as they could through wholesalers and then they'd gather the odds and ends at commercial, big-box stores. Before this experience, Chas had no idea of the amount of work that went into planning a dinner party. It was impressive how efficient and thorough Ryleigh was. She pretty much had everything under control.

Adrenaline pulsed through Chas as he pulled up in front of Ryleigh's house. He felt like he was on the one-yard line, about to blast through the goal line for a touchdown. The fact that Ryleigh had agreed to let him pick her up at her house spoke volumes. From here, they were off to the airport. Originally, he'd told Ryleigh that they'd fly out this evening. However, the best option for flights was to take a nonstop that left Dallas at one pm. Chas didn't mind leaving earlier. That meant more time with Ryleigh. He was looking forward to introducing her to his family, especially his parents. He suspected that Ryleigh and his mom would get along well.

Ryleigh lived in a middle-class neighborhood of modest ranch style homes built in the 1980s. The house was a beige brick with dusty blue shutters. The landscaping was simple, yet well-kept. As he got out of the car, and strode up the walkway, he felt movement from behind. He turned sharply, flinching when he realized there was a man close behind him.

"Hey," Chas said with a startled laugh. "I didn't see you there." Chills of having been taken unaware raced down his spine.

The guy stepped up to him. He was about an inch shorter than Chas with a wiry build. For a second, Chas was caught off guard by the animosity emanating from the man whose dark eyes flickered over Chas. Instinctively, Chas straightened to his full height, his jaw pulling tight. "I'm sorry. Do I know you?"

"Joe Martin." His chest expanded like a proud rooster.

For a second, the name didn't register. Then it clicked. "Joey," he said aloud, the hair on his neck bristling. Had Joey come here today for a fight? It certainly seemed that way. Chas was struck by how much Noah looked like his dad. Same dark, spiky hair, same eyes. No surprise. Joey was a good-looking guy, but he had trouble written all over him—the type of guy who thought the world should roll out the red carpet because of his looks. "I'm—"

"I know who you are," Joey cut in. "The hotshot football player. You think you're something with your fancy car and fat paycheck, don't you, pretty boy?"

Chas balled his fist. The last thing he wanted today was a fight, especially with Ryleigh's ex and Noah's father. It wouldn't take much to lay this weasel out flat. Then again, while Chas could easily win the battle, socking Joey would lose him the war. Ryleigh would never forgive him, which is probably what Joey was counting on. With a superhuman effort, Chas released his fist, smiling. "Ryleigh told me about you."

"Is that so?" Joey fired back.

"Yeah, how you have a hard time holding down a job."

Joey's mouth went slack.

Chas leaned forward, his voice going hard. "Even worse, how you told your own son a bunch of garbage to manipulate him and Ryleigh. That's pathetic, man."

Fury streaked through Joey's eyes. He swore under his breath, looking like he was about to lose it.

"Go ahead," Chas taunted. "Give it your best shot."

The door opened. "What's going on?" Ryleigh asked, eyes wide as saucers.

Joey was the first to speak. "Your boy and I were just getting acquainted."

Chas laughed. "Is that what you call this?"

"What're you doing here, Joey?" Ryleigh demanded, giving him a scathing look. "Did you come here to cause trouble?"

He held up his hands, his voice going innocent. "No, babe, I stopped by to pick up Noah's glove. That way, I'll have it when I pick him up from school this afternoon. We're going directly to the park."

Chas cringed hearing Joey call Ryleigh *babe*. He expected—hoped—Ryleigh would call Joey out about it, but she didn't. Instead, she folded her arms over her chest, giving Joey a long, hard look. "All right," she finally said, her voice cracking like a whip. "I'll get the glove and then you can be on your way."

"Thank you," Joey said breezily. When Ryleigh went back inside, Joey turned to Chas. "Let me tell you how this is gonna go," he said in a low tone. "You'll whisk her off to New Orleans and romance her for a few days, but in the end, I'll win her back." A triumphant smile twisted over his lips. "I always win."

Disgust settled like a slab of concrete in Chas's gut. "You're not a winner. You let the most amazing woman on the planet slip through your fingers. You let Ryleigh down, betrayed her trust." He locked gazes with the scumbag. "What you are is history."

Rage boiled in Joey's eyes. He let out a string of curses and drew back his fist like he was going to strike.

"Go ahead," Chas said calmly.

Joey backed down, breathing heavily. "You watch yourself," he warned, clenching his jaw.

Ryleigh returned with the glove and tossed it to Joey. "The plan is for you to take Noah to the park and then bring him home no later than four. Tess will take over from there." She pinned him with a look. "Is that understood?"

"Yeah, babe, I've got it." A grin snaked over his mouth, his eyes glittering as he cast a mocking glance at Chas.

"Cut the crap, Joey. I'm not your babe. You and I both know it," Ryleigh said. Her voice sounded more tired and frustrated than angry.

Joey's smile faltered for a second before he cinched it back up. "Sorry, old habits die hard. Nice to meet you, Chas," he said pleasantly. Then he leaned in and uttered in a low tone, "Remember what I said." He turned back to Ryleigh as he saluted. "See ya, Ry." With that, he strutted away.

"Hey," Ryleigh said when Chas approached. "Sorry about that." She rolled her eyes. "I had no idea he was going to show up here."

Tension pulled tight against his shoulders. "No worries. I'm glad I finally got to put a face with the reputation."

She tipped her head, worry darkening her eyes. "What did he say to you?"

"Nothing of consequence." No way was he going to let Joey ruin this trip. A smile tugged at his lips. "You look incredible ... as always."

"Thanks," she murmured demurely, her lashes brushing softly against her cheekbones in that subtle way he loved. Right there on the doorstep, he slid an arm around her waist and kissed her lips. She pulled back, embarrassed. "I'm sure you're giving the neighbors something to talk about." She glanced around.

"I hope so," he drawled, winking. "How's the packing going?"

"I'm about ready. Just putting the last few things in my suitcase. Come on in."

As Chas stepped in and closed the door, he pushed away the remains of the dark mood that Joey had created. Chas meant what he said. While Joey was Noah's father and therefore a fixed part of Ryleigh's life, Joey was history as far as his relationship with Ryleigh was concerned. Chas was Ryleigh's present, and he had every intention of doing everything in his power to ensure that he was a part of her future.

RYLEIGH WAS SO nervous she was shaky. She knew it showed. Concern flickered in Chas's bright blue eyes. "Are you doing okay?"

She squeezed his hand, forcing a smile. "I'm fine." They were in a rental car, driving to his family's home.

"They're gonna love you," he said with a reassuring smile. He laughed to himself. "How could they not?" He cast her a sidelong glance. "I already do."

She sucked in a quick breath, catching the meaning of his statement. No way could Chas love her. It was too soon in their relationship for that.

He seemed to be reading her thoughts as a laugh lighter than a summer's breeze floated from his throat. "Don't worry, I'm not trying to pin you against the wall for a commitment. I'll wait until the four months are up for that."

She blinked a few times, a hesitant laugh gurgling in her throat. Then she got a good look at his expression. "You're teasing me, aren't you?"

A crooked grin slid over his lips. "Just trying to lighten the mood a little."

She let out a long breath. "I'm sorry. I shouldn't be so keyed up. I just want to make sure I do a good job for the family dinner. It is for your family, after all." *And, I want to make a good impression on them personally.* Chas had told her he was falling hard for her. Well, the same was happening on her end. It was both scary and thrilling. When Chas invited her to go to New Orleans with him, she'd been ecstatic. Tess readily agreed to watch Noah. Gemma even offered to help. Then, Joey stopped by the house, and Noah had told him about the trip. That's when Joey insisted on taking Noah to the park and out for ice cream. Ryleigh couldn't remember the last time Joey had taken Noah to the park.

It was obvious that Joey felt threatened by Chas. Ryleigh could tell that words had passed between the two. She could tell that Joey had said something snarky to Chas. To Chas's credit, he kept his cool. Joey was becoming a huge pain! She wasn't sure what to do about him. For so long, she'd allowed him to just come and go as he pleased. With Chas in the picture, that would have to stop.

They pulled into an upscale, historical section of town.

"This is Esplanade Avenue. It runs through the heart of the city, from the Mississippi River to City Park."

"It seems so quiet and serene," Ryleigh said with a sense of awe, "like we've gone back in time." Her gaze swept over the brightly colored, venerable houses decked to the nines with their large, beveled-glass windows and intricate architectural features. "What kind of trees are those?" A light-gray, furry moss hung from the branches, almost as though someone had artfully placed it there.

"Majestic Oaks. All right. Here we are," Chas announced.

Ryleigh's eyes bugged as she pointed to the grand, olive-tone home with the neat rows of windows, flanked by aged, black shutters. "That's your family's home?"

"Yep," Chas answered, pride sounding in his voice.

"It's incredible," Ryleigh uttered, clutching her throat. Ryleigh was way out of her league. Her heart drummed out a ragged beat as she swallowed.

He stopped alongside the road, directly in front of the house. "It's called a side hall home because the front is built so close to the street."

"Almost like a townhouse in New York," she observed.

He pointed to the right-hand section off to the side. The structure was separate with its own roof, but connected at the bottom by a wall of two doors. "That's the guest quarters," he explained, "where you'll stay."

Her own quarters? Her eyes widened.

"The home was built in the 1860s. It's Greek Revival style."

She nodded like she knew, although she had very little knowledge of architecture. All she knew was that this mansion was grander than anything she could've imagined. Mostly because it represented an elegant slice of history. The kind of people who lived in this neighborhood had understated wealth built upon several generations ... or at least that was Ryleigh's impression. "I can see why you chose to live in the historical section of Ft. Worth."

He grinned. "It was about as close to home as I could get in Texas."

They pulled into the side driveway and drove around to the back of the home. "They left the gates open for us," Chas said as he pulled into a large courtyard surrounded by high walls. "It looks like everyone's already here."

She gave him a questioning look.

"My brothers and sister."

There were several other cars, all luxury—BMWs, a Lexus, a Range Rover, and a red, convertible Porsche.

"My sister's car," Chas said, as if reading her mind. "She opted for the red to match her nickname."

"Huh?"

"Red. That's what we call her."

"Oh." How was Ryleigh supposed to find common ground with these wealthy, privileged people?

"Don't get that door," Chas quipped as he darted out in quick, nimble movements. With flair, he opened her door, a broad smile on his handsome face. "I can't wait to show you off. Let's go in and say hello, then I'll come back out to get the luggage."

"You mean you don't have servants for that?" she joked, then regretted her words when she saw his crestfallen expression.

He was quick to recover as he smiled. "Nope, just me."

"I'm sorry." She coughed to clear the frog in her throat. "This is a lot to take in."

He caught hold of her hand, frowning. "You're as cold as ice."

She forced a smile. "I'm good. Once the introductions are over with I'll settle down. I'm not used to large families, remember?"

"That's true," he conceded, giving her a perceptive look. "Is that all that's wrong? You're so edgy."

Her lips drew into a tight line. "I've got a lot of loose ends to pull together for the party."

He pulled her close, planting a kiss on her cheek. "Don't worry, I'll help. I'm your humble servant," he uttered huskily, "here to assist in whatever way you should need."

The flicker of desire in his beautiful eyes sent warmth rushing through her as she laughed. "That's good to know." The banter helped put her at ease as they walked through the back door. Her jitters returned with a vengeance when she saw the inside of the home with the tall ceilings and detailed moldings. "This is incredible," she breathed, soaking everything in like a sponge as they walked across the glossy wood floors that creaked pleasantly beneath their feet.

They came into a large, modern kitchen. The cabinets were a rich mahogany that contrasted nicely with the vivid orange-red walls. Black granite veined in delicate strands of white adorned the countertops, and the gas cooktop and oven were encased in a magnificent brick edifice painted a taupe color. Excitement trickled over her. This is where she would prepare the food for the party.

"Hello," Chas called loudly, his commanding voice echoing through the large space. "Anyone home?"

"In the den," a female voice answered.

Ryleigh's heart hammered against her chest as they stepped in. Her eyes made a quick sweep over the room, not really seeing anyone as she plastered a friendly smile over her face.

"Everybody, this is Ryleigh Eisenhart," he boomed like she was a celebrity.

15

Chas's mom was the first to approach. Ryleigh was struck by the uncommon beauty of the tall, slender woman with short, dark hair, tapered and wispy around her face.

"Hello," she said regally, taking Ryleigh's hand and pulling her into a hug. Ryleigh caught a whiff of her expensive perfume. She pulled back, her crystal blue eyes assessing Ryleigh. "I'm Effie."

"It's nice to meet you," Ryleigh said, trying to sound more confident than she felt.

A warm smile spread over Effie's features. "Thanks so much for organizing the dinner. You're a lifesaver."

"I'm glad to help."

Effie looked at Chas, her features glowing. "It's good to see you, son." She gave him a tight hug, holding onto him for a second like she was breathing him in.

"Good to see you too, Mom."

After the hug, Chas stepped close to Ryleigh and put a protective arm around her. She was grateful for his support. Her knees felt wobblier than a bowl of Jell-O.

A stunning redhead with a mane of long, wavy hair bounded up. "Hello, I'm McKenna," she chimed, "Chas's favorite sister."

"My only sister," Chas corrected, with an amused grin.

McKenna lifted her chin. "That's why I'm the favorite."

Ryleigh extended her hand, thinking they'd shake, but McKenna hugged her instead.

"It's nice to meet you," she said exuberantly. She drew back, making a point of looking Ryleigh up and down. "You're a beauty."

"Thank you. So are you," Ryleigh said sincerely.

Appreciation flashed in McKenna's eyes. "Thank you," she sang before grabbing Chas in a tight hug. "How are ya, bro? It has been too long."

"Yes, it has," Chas agreed.

Mischief danced across McKenna's features. "So, you brought a girl home," she drawled. "It's about time."

Ryleigh was surprised by that ... and pleased. She looked at Chas whose face had turned crimson. It was cute to see him blush.

"Ah," McKenna teased, "you like her, a lot."

A guy who looked remarkably like Chas stepped up and extended his hand. "Hey, I'm Caden." He gave her a firm shake.

Caden's freckles were a little more prominent than Chas's, and his hair was buzzed. He was a little shorter and more muscular. She caught the same confident glimmer in his blue-green eyes as Chas. She got the impression that Caden was soft-spoken.

McKenna draped an arm around Caden's shoulders. "I know it looks like Caden is Chas's twin, but he's really mine."

The playful manner with which she said it made Ryleigh think she was joking. Then, she remembered that there was a set of twins. She could tell from the look on Caden's face that it was true.

"Caden thinks he's a stud muffin because of his military background and the fact that he works for a kick butt security group." Her eyes danced. "But I'd put my skills up against his any day."

"Red is a private detective," Chas said, exchanging an amused look with Caden. "Sounds like she's getting a little too big for her britches."

Caden quirked a grin, chuckling. The mannerism was so like Chas that Ryleigh did a double take.

"Hey," McKenna protested, her hands going to her hips.

"Now, children," Effie chided. "You've only been together a short while. Don't start fighting." Her voice held the controlled edge of one accustomed to keeping the peace.

Everyone laughed.

Chas turned to the tall, angular-faced man who'd stepped up. He was dressed in casual business attire and unlike his other siblings had a solemn demeanor. He, too, was handsome in a professor, bookish way. Chas motioned. "This is my older brother Colin."

Colin offered a curt nod. "Nice to meet you."

"Nice to meet you too," Ryleigh repeated dutifully. Something in the cool way Colin's eyes assessed her let her know that she didn't measure up.

Chas gave Colin a hug. For an instant, Colin stood awkwardly before returning the hug.

"Colin works in finance," Chas said, his hand resting on Colin's shoulder. He made a face. "Don't ask me anymore because that's all I know."

McKenna hooted. "Join the club." She shoved Colin who stood stiffly as if an invisible barrier kept him from fully interacting with his siblings. "None of the rest of us have big enough brains to understand the important work he does. Isn't that right, Colin?" she taunted.

A deep flush came over Colin's face. Ryleigh could tell that McKenna was picking up an ongoing argument between her and Colin.

"Enough," Colin warned, shooting her a dark look, but she only laughed and blew him a kiss.

"Quit taunting your brother," Effie warned. She let out an exasperated sigh, giving Ryleigh an apologetic look. "You sure you're up for spending the weekend with this motley bunch?"

Chas caressed her with a gaze. "Ryleigh's tough. She can handle it."

The confidence in his tone bolstered her courage as she stood up straighter. "Yes," she answered, a smile ruffling her lips. "I'm up for the challenge."

"I like you already," McKenna said. She brought her hands together, eyes sparkling. "Chas said I can help you with the party."

Ryleigh's eyes cut to Chas. He tugged at his sweater, laughing nervously. "I hope it was okay. McKenna really wants to help."

All eyes went to Ryleigh. McKenna seemed like a fun, larger-than-life personality. Ryleigh wasn't sure how easy she'd be to work with, or how well she would follow orders. Still, what other choice did she have at this point but to let her help? "Of course," she said smoothly.

"Awesome!" McKenna beamed.

Ryleigh shot Chas an irritated look, letting him know she didn't appreciate him bringing McKenna into the dinner prep without asking her first.

Chas glanced around the room. "Where's Gram, Asher and Dad?"

"Gram's taking a nap," Caden said. "She wanted to be rested before tonight."

"Asher's practicing with his band and Dad's still at work," McKenna piped in.

Effie frowned. "Hopefully, they'll be home before too long. We have dinner reservations at the club for six."

"Is Asher in a band?" Chas asked dubiously. He turned to Ryleigh. "He's the youngest of the O'Brien clan."

Effie nodded. "They've been playing at different locations around the city."

Chas made a face. "Are they any good?" This elicited a snigger from McKenna.

"Surprisingly, yes," Caden answered.

Chas cocked his head. "What does Asher play?"

"Keyboards and guitar," Effie said.

Chas pursed his lips. "Who knew?" He looked at Ryleigh. "Well, let's get you settled and then I'll get your luggage."

"I can help," Caden offered.

Effie smiled. "Ryleigh, we're so glad you're here. Please let me know if you need anything."

"Thank you." Ryleigh liked Effie most of all. She was the picture of grace, but had a quiet strength about her. It was obvious that she fiercely loved her children. A pang went through her. What she would've given for a mother like that. Chas didn't know how lucky he was to have grown up here.

"What can I do to help with the dinner?" McKenna asked eagerly.

"Down girl," Chas said with a laugh. "I want Ryleigh to have some relaxing time before she dives into work tomorrow. I'm gonna show Ryleigh the city and then we'll meet y'all at the club."

McKenna frowned. "All right. But tomorrow, I'm in full force." She looked at Chas, daring him to disagree.

"I'm sure there will be plenty for you to do," Chas said evenly, glancing at Ryleigh.

"Yes." Ryleigh forced a smile. "Tomorrow will be a busy day. It'll be nice to have your help."

"Fantastic!" McKenna said with gusto. The corners of her lips turned down. "I've been going crazy all day, trying to find things to keep myself occupied."

"You could resume your favorite past-time of spying on the neighbors," Colin said.

When Caden sniggered, McKenna popped him on the arm.

"Ouch!" he complained, holding his arm. "What was that for?"

"I don't spy on the neighbors ... anymore," she retorted, her cheeks going red. She stuck her tongue out at Colin. "You're an idiot!"

Colin didn't crack a smile, just stared back at her with a deadpan expression.

Ryleigh looked at Chas who had laughter in his eyes. "McKenna has always had a keen interest in everyone and everything around her. Before she honed her skills and put them to work as a PI, she used to cut her teeth on the neighbors."

Caden hooted. "Remember when you thought that Mr. Greenshaw was laundering money because he was carrying out garbage bags in the middle of the night?" His eyes held laughter as he looked at Ryleigh. "Turns out he was just cleaning out his closet. The poor man couldn't sleep, so he was carrying out bags to donate to the thrift store."

McKenna thrust out her lower lip in a pout. "Well, it was suspicious. Who carries out garbage bags in the middle of the night to take to a thrift store?"

"Mr. Greenshaw," Chas and Caden said simultaneously.

Even Effie was trying not to smile. "All right boys. That's enough."

"As exciting as this has been, I've got to make a few phone calls before dinner," Colin said briskly, striding out.

McKenna wrinkled her nose. "Is it just my imagination, or does he seem more uptight than usual?"

"McKenna," Effie blurted. "Enough of that! You know how hard it has been on Colin since his divorce. Cut him some slack."

"All right, but only because it's your birthday on Saturday," McKenna huffed. "Colin has always been a stuffed shirt. I swear, if you pull up his hundred-dollar silk shirt, you'll see a board attached to his spine."

The corners of Ryleigh's lips twitched. She tried hard to squelch the laughter, but it came out as a short burst.

"What?" McKenna asked, also laughing.

"You remind me of my sister."

McKenna's brows creased. "Is that a good or bad thing?"

"A very good thing," Chas said so quickly that it sounded like he was overcompensating.

Suspicion crept into McKenna's expression.

"It's a very good thing," Ryleigh assured her. "My sister's great." Tess was great, although she could pester the hind legs off a donkey. Much the same way McKenna was doing. Speaking of Tess, she wondered how things were going back home. As soon as Ryleigh got to her room, she'd call to make sure that Joey had dropped Noah off like he was supposed to. Joey had been acting so strange lately that it made her nervous to let Noah go off with him alone. Then again, it was tricky to avoid it since Joey was his father and had visitation rights.

Chas motioned with his head. "Let's go."

As Ryleigh and Chas stepped outside the room, she halted when she heard McKenna's comment. "She's impressive."

Chas gave a look filled with so much adoration that it caused her heart to flip. "See, I told you they'd love you."

Warmth flooded Ryleigh. "I like them too." She frowned. "Colin's interesting."

Chas's eyes tightened around the edges. "Yeah, he's a bit of a wet noodle, I'm afraid."

"I don't think he likes me very much."

He grunted. "Colin doesn't like anyone, not even himself."

"So, he's divorced?"

"Yeah, he and Beverly split up a little over a year ago."

She shook her head. "That's too bad."

They were in the hallway, leading out to the back door. Chas stopped in his tracks, giving her a funny look. "Not getting any ideas about trading me in for Colin, are you?"

She laughed in surprise. "I wouldn't trade you in for ten Colins."

His azure eyes twinkled as his arm encircled her waist, pulling her closer. "Only ten?" he murmured in her ear, his breath sending tantalizing shivers down her spine.

"A hundred!"

Warm laughter flowed out of him, encircling her like a cocoon. "You really are something," he uttered, his eyes moving over her in a slow, leisurely way that sizzled her blood. "I can't wait to get you in the guest room so I can have you all to myself."

Her eyes seemed to have a mind of their own as they went to his lips. She was close to kissing him then and there, but then remembered where they were. She glanced around, heat creeping up her neck. "Maybe we should wait until we're alone, before ..." She knew her face was flaming like a neon sign, especially when she saw Chas's quirky grin letting her know he knew the effect he had on her.

He laughed, reluctantly releasing her. "Good idea."

"I'll help you get the luggage out." She flashed a coquettish grin, batting her eyelashes. "It's the least I can do since you don't have a servant at your beck and call."

He looked around. "Hey, that's right. Caden said he'd help. Where is that slacker?"

"Slacker's right here," Caden said. He grinned as Ryleigh and Chas pulled apart.

"Hey, Ryleigh," Caden began innocent-eyed. "Did you say you had a sister?"

"Yes," she answered, not sure where this was going.

A cocky grin slid over Caden's lips. "Is she as pretty as you?"

Ryleigh's face flamed even more. She'd pegged Caden as soft-spoken, but he was more forthright than she gave him credit for.

Chas stepped behind Ryleigh and slid his arms around her shoulders. His voice took on the languid tone of a cowboy, "Now, don't be hitting on my girl."

Caden held up both hands. "I wouldn't dream of it, bro," he chuckled. "I was just thinking I'd like to meet Ryleigh's sister."

Ryleigh realized then that this had nothing to with her or Tess, per se, but was a form of teasing. She laughed, getting caught up in the light-hearted banter between the brothers. "You could meet Tess, but you'd be doing so at your own risk. Tess is a pistol."

A full smile spread over Caden's lips. "I like her already." He motioned. "Lead the way," he winked at Ryleigh, "to the luggage. The sister will have to wait."

16

For the formal dinner, Ryleigh chose to make roasted chicken with risotto and caramelized onions. The beef option was tenderloin with a red wine, mushroom sauce, complimented by creamy mashed potatoes. She'd started the dinner with an array of appetizers and followed this with a spinach salad, complimented with pears, red onion, cranberries, and toasted pine nuts. Both entrees were accompanied with fresh cranberry salad and a medley of tender green beans and carrots. For dessert, the guests had a choice of either key lime pie or a rich devil's food layer cake.

Ryleigh assumed that she, Chas, and McKenna would be the ones serving dinner. However, she was pleasantly surprised to learn that Chas's dad Griffin hired a staff to serve and clean up. While she didn't voice it out loud, Ryleigh feared hiring the staff of six would eat into her profit, but Chas assured her that she'd still be paid the five thousand, as promised. Chas was so good to her that Ryleigh could hardly believe he was real.

No, she could hardly believe this night was real. Everything had gone off without a hitch as if touched by magic. McKenna had been a big help, and she didn't mind following orders in the least. It had been good to have a woman's help. Chas meant well, but he didn't know the first thing about food prep. She laughed inwardly thinking of how he'd bungled around the kitchen, eating almost as much of the food as he chopped. Still, she was so grateful for his effort and how much he cared.

A feeling of pride touched Ryleigh as she looked around at the magnificent dining room. She'd snapped a few pictures for Tess and her portfolio at the start of the party. Ryleigh had a handful of trusted clients, but she'd never done an event of this magnitude before. The long walnut table was decked out with the finest table settings that Ryleigh had ever seen. The flicker of the candles cast a golden glow over the room. Ryleigh's gaze took in the lavish silk window drapes, moving up to the enormous, glittering chandelier overhead.

The easy chatter of conversation floated just above the volume of the classical music playing softly in the background. Ryleigh enjoyed watching Chas's parents. It was obvious that Griffin doted on Effie. Big and muscular with a shock of silver hair, Griffin was a handsome man with his even features and light, lively eyes.

Looking at Shannon Chas's grandmother, it was easy to see the Irish influence. Her hair was a couple shades darker than McKenna's, and it was streaked with silver. Shannon had milky skin and a smattering of freckles. She had an infectious laugh and loved to be the center of conversation. Her Irish brogue had a lyrical, ethereal quality, which made Ryleigh want to just sit and listen to her talk all day. Feeling Ryleigh's eyes on her, Shannon flashed a wide smile, lighting her entire face.

Asher, the youngest brother, sat on Shannon's left. With his stylishly cut blonde hair and O'Brien blue eyes, he was charming but had a rebel edge to him. Ryleigh could picture him being in a band.

Chas slid an arm around her shoulders. "You outdid yourself."

"Thank you," she murmured.

"There's only one problem," he said, patting his stomach. "I couldn't decide if I wanted the beef or chicken, so I had to try both."

Ryleigh laughed as she reached for Chas's hand underneath the table and linked her fingers through his. "It has been a wonderful visit." She enjoyed the quick tour of New Orleans that Chas had given her Thursday evening. The old-world charm was alive and well in New Orleans. Surprisingly, Ryleigh even enjoyed dinner at the country club, mostly because she liked listening to Griffin's jokes.

Griffin pinged his glass. "May I have everyone's attention?" he asked loudly.

The table quieted down as all eyes turned to him.

Griffin turned to Effie. "Happy birthday to my exquisite angel. She captured my heart the first moment I laid eyes on her, and she's never let it go. Effie, you are even more beautiful now than you were the day I met you. Happy birthday, darling. May there be many more wonderful days ahead." He raised his glass.

Pleased murmurs rippled around the table as everyone lifted their glasses.

"Oh," Griffin said, meeting Ryleigh's eyes across the table. "A special thanks to the lovely Ryleigh Eisenhart." He grinned. "Not only has she accomplished the nearly impossible feat of capturing my son's heart, but she's prepared this delicious meal. I'm sure we'll be seeing much more of Ryleigh in the future."

Ryleigh blinked in surprise, heat fanning her cheeks. "Thank you."

Effie nodded, offering a smile that seemed to echo everything Griffin had just said.

"Amen to that," Chas uttered in her ear.

A glow of contentment settled over Ryleigh. Crazy that she would feel so comfortable here with these powerful, dynamic people. Maybe this is what family actually felt like. More than anything she wished Noah and Tess were here so they could experience it too.

After the party was over, Ryleigh found herself in the living room with Effie while Chas went out to play a game of basketball with Caden and Asher.

"Thank you again for such a wonderful evening." Effie grinned. "I panicked when I found out the caterer had fallen through. Then, Chas told us about you." She gave Ryleigh a significant look. "Chas thinks the world of you."

"I think the world of him too."

Effie's eyes probed hers for a long moment. "Yes, I believe you do," she said decisively. She tipped her head sideways, pursing her lips as if she were trying to decide how much she wanted to say to Ryleigh. "Chas's football has made it hard for him to find someone ... er, to know if the woman he's with truly cares about him."

Ryleigh went cold. Was Effie implying that Ryleigh wanted Chas for his celebrity status? Her heart began to pound.

Effie put a hand over Ryleigh's. "I'm only telling you this because I can see that you do care about Chas. Not about the player, but him."

"I do," Ryleigh answered firmly so there would be no question about her intentions.

"Chas has never brought anyone home before. That's why Griffin said in his toast that you'd accomplished the impossible of capturing Chas's heart."

Ryleigh loved the sound of that. She smiled inwardly thinking how Chas had seemed like he was way out of her league, and now here she was in the home where he grew up having a heart-to-heart with his mother. Her life was turning out so much better than she could've ever dared to hope.

Effie's face softened, peeling away the years so that she looked a decade younger. "Tell me about your son."

Ryleigh was surprised that Effie knew about Noah.

"Chas and I are very close," Effie said as if answering her unspoken thoughts. "He told me about the ball and how he rescued Noah."

"I'm so glad Chas was there." Ryleigh shuddered. "I hate even thinking about what might've happened otherwise."

Effie nodded in understanding. "Trust me, I know how rambunctious boys can be."

"Yes, I'm sure you do." Ryleigh could only imagine how hectic things must've been in this household with so many boys. Ryleigh rattled off a few tidbits about Noah, impressed with how Effie seemed so genuinely interested.

A few minutes later, Effie sighed. "I'm looking forward to meeting Noah. I hope you'll bring him the next time you come to visit."

Contentment rippled through Ryleigh. "Yes, that would be great." Effie was speaking in future tense, as if Ryleigh would be included in that future.

Effie looked thoughtful, like a new thought had suddenly occurred to her. "There's something I want to give you, a small token of my appreciation for tonight."

"Oh, that's not necessary," Ryleigh countered, but her protest fell on deaf ears as Effie stood, waving a hand.

"I'll be right back."

She returned a minute later and sat back down in the same spot. "Here." She handed the item to Ryleigh.

Ryleigh gulped as she looked down and realized she was holding a Prada handbag. It looked expensive, over a thousand dollars expensive.

Hope gleamed in Effie's eyes. "Do you like it?"

"Yeah." She ran her hand over the smooth, champagne leather, taking note of the fine stitching along the edges. "It's beautiful."

Effie flashed a toothy smile. "I'm glad."

"I can't accept it." She shook her head. "It's too much." *Geez.* She'd just had the same conversation with Chas. The apple didn't fall far from the tree.

"Of course you can," Effie countered with a feather-light laugh. "It's a party favor left over from a luncheon that I hosted for my girlfriends. It's just been laying around here, collecting dust. I want you to have it."

A Prada bag as a party favor? Who could afford to give a party favor that extravagant?

"Please take it." The pleading expression on Effie's face was the same one Chas used. Ryleigh could no more turn Effie down than she could Chas.

"Okay. Thank you," she said mechanically.

Effie's shoulders relaxed.

A few beats of awkward silence passed until Effie spoke. "How do you come up with your recipes? That food was delicious."

"Thank you." Ryleigh could tell that Effie was searching for a conversation topic. She was happy to talk about something that she knew. Effie's phone rang. She held up a manicured finger. "Excuse me for a minute."

"Of course."

The peace that Ryleigh had been experiencing vanished as the old fears resurged. Regardless of how comfortable Ryleigh had felt around Chas's family earlier, the stark truth hit her square between the eyes as she looked down at the Prada bag.

She and the O'Briens were worlds apart.

17

Except for those few moments when Effie gave Ryleigh the Prada handbag, it had been a wonderful trip. Ryleigh had been rattled by the expensive bag, then Chas strode into the living room with a confident, springy bounce. His eyes caught hers in a long, tender gaze, restoring her confidence. Sweaty and all, he'd sat down close and placed an arm around her. A few minutes later, Griffin came in. The four of them talked for several hours. Finally, after their tongues waxed tired and everyone started yawning, Ryleigh concluded that, yes, she and the O'Briens were different, but that was okay. She couldn't deny that being with Chas felt like coming home. It was a feeling she'd never experienced before, but it was wonderful—something she could get used to.

"After having you to myself the past few days, I hate to give you up," Chas lamented as he pulled in front of her house.

She laughed, feeling deliriously happy. "It's only until tomorrow." They'd planned to have lunch together at Chas's house in between client appointments.

Chas blew out a labored sigh. "I guess I have no choice but to wait." There were traces of humor around his eyes and mouth. He angled to face her. "Thank you for everything."

She marveled at the inherent strength he exuded, her eyes tracing the chiseled lines of his features. For an instant, she got lost in the vivid color of his blue eyes. She cupped his lean jaw. "Thank you."

He leaned over and claimed her lips with a long, passionate kiss that sang bliss through her veins and left her mouth burning with fire. When he pulled back, he gazed at her with such tenderness that she thought she'd melt. "I love you," he admitted.

She jerked, her eyes flying open wide. Her pulse shot through the roof of the car. The most incredible man she'd ever met just told her he loved her.

His lips curved in gentle laughter. "Don't worry. I'm not expecting a response right now. I just wanted you to know."

"What about the four-month rule?"

He broke into a full smile. "Hang the four-month rule. What's four months in comparison to the real deal?"

A burst of pure, undiluted happiness glowed through her like sunshine finally breaking through the thick, immovable clouds. She couldn't stop the bubble of laughter that issued from her lips. She felt reckless, happy, like anything was possible. "Hey, I know we planned to meet for lunch tomorrow, but how would you feel about changing the plans to dinner?"

"Even better."

"At my house, with Noah."

He blinked, rewarding her with a smile so dazzling it rivaled the sun. "I would love that."

"Me too."

He stroked her hair. "Thank you for coming into my life," he uttered.

"Thank you for making the impossible possible."

He laughed. "I guess it was meant to be."

"Yes, it was."

He sighed. "All right. I guess I need to help you get your luggage inside." He gave her a perceptive look. "As much as you're enjoying spending time with me, I know you're ready to see Noah."

"I am," she admitted, a smile stretching over her face. "I missed the little stinker."

Chas helped her to the door, then leaned in and planted a soft, velvety peck on her lips. "Hopefully, that won't get the neighbors in too much of an uproar," he joked, then turned, walking back to his car with long, fluid strides. Before he got in, he flashed a disarming smile that flipped her stomach. She watched as he drove away, wondering how she'd ever gotten so lucky.

"I'M THINKING about inviting Chas over for dinner tonight," Ryleigh said casually the next morning over breakfast.

Tess's eyes rounded, then an incredulous smile spread over her lips. "Really? That's great!" A coy expression came over her. "I take it things went well in New Orleans?"

"You could say that," Ryleigh said, unable to contain the giant smile that pulled at her lips. She curled her fingers around her warm mug of herbal tea.

"I'm glad, sis." Tess paused. "So, do you think Chas will pay you the extra ten thousand for doing the dinner?"

Ryleigh scowled. "I hope not. I told him not to."

"You're so dang stubborn," Tess pouted. "That ten thousand would help us tremendously."

"Griffin, Chas's dad, wrote me a check for five thousand."

Tess's voice lifted. "Oh, good." She rolled her eyes. "At least you had the good sense to take that."

"Whatever," Ryleigh responded dryly. She'd not yet told Tess about the Prada bag. Tess would freak, probably try to claim it for herself. Ryleigh stood, taking a sip of her tea as she glanced at the clock. "I'd better get Noah up and ready for school. Thanks again for taking care of him while I was gone."

Tess waved a hand. "No worries. We had fun. Gemma was a big help. We spent all Saturday with her and Doug. Their grandkids were in town. Noah loved playing with them."

"That's awesome. How did it go with Joey?" She tensed.

"Good, because I only saw him once, the day he brought Noah home from the park." Tess's upper lip curled in disdain. "The less we see of him the better."

Ryleigh was inclined to agree, but she didn't want to voice it out loud. She was trying to cut Joey as much slack as she could, but his actions were making it difficult. She took one last drink of the tea and dumped the remainder in the sink as she pulled her robe tighter around her, yawning. "It's hard to jump back into the swing of things right after a trip."

"Oh, stop your whining," Tess chided. "It's a rough life, getting whisked away to New Orleans for the weekend, flying first class, with your celebrity boyfriend. Whaaa!"

Ryleigh wrinkled her nose. "Yeah, it's a rough life, but somebody's gotta do it," she quipped as she waltzed into the other room to wake up Noah.

An hour later, she'd just gotten back from dropping Noah off at school and was doing some research for dishes to make for the Grilling and Chilling Cooking Competition when the doorbell rang. Tess had already left to deposit Griffin's check and make a grocery store run before they were to meet at a client's home. The doorbell rang again as Ryleigh went to the door. Her heart sank when she looked through the peep hole and realized it was Joey. She didn't have time for this today.

Joey rapped hard on the door. "Open up, Ryleigh. I know you're home."

She and Tess had decided to start locking the front door so Joey couldn't just waltz in whenever he pleased. She placed a hand against the door, blowing out a long breath. Finally, she opened the door. "I don't have a lot of time today, Joey," she grumbled, then gasped when she looked at him. "W—what happened to you?"

His head was shaved. His eyes were solemn, the corners of his lips turning down. "There's something I need to tell you."

She swallowed, uneasiness trickling down her spine.

He motioned. "May I come in?"

"Sure, but like I said, I'm in a hurry." It was startling to see Joey bald. His egg-shaped head was stark white, giving his face an odd, sunken appearance.

"This won't take long."

He went to the couch and sat down. She chose the chair across from him. He clasped his hands tightly in his lap. She could feel the nervous energy oozing off him.

She leaned forward in her seat, her stomach twisting in a hard knot. "Joey, what's wrong?"

He looked down at his hands.

"Joey!" she prompted, irritation pricking over her. Was this some sort of game?

His face lifted. Tears brimmed in his eyes as his lower lip trembled. "I—I'm afraid I have some bad news."

Ryleigh's world shattered in the wake of his next words. Her hands began to shake as she pinched the bridge of her nose, tears streaming down her face.

The beautiful dream was over.

CHAS HAD JUST FINISHED his workout and was in the kitchen taking a long drink of water when the doorbell rang. He went to answer it.

"Hey, this is a nice surprise," he boomed with a large smile. His heart lurched when he saw Ryleigh's red-rimmed eyes and stricken expression. "What's wrong?"

"We need to talk," she said hoarsely.

"Sure, come on in." He led her into the den where they sat down. He touched her hands, which were ice. Panic swept through him like a tidal wave. "What's wrong? Did something happen to Noah?" Please let Noah be okay, he prayed. It would destroy Ryleigh if anything ever happened to him.

"No, Noah's fine." Ryleigh's lips pressed into a tight line. Her face was alabaster.

"What's wrong?" Chas put a hand on her arm. He wanted to pull her into his arms and smooth away the stress lines from her beautiful face, but he sensed that Ryleigh needed her space. The raw anguish in her eyes sliced ribbons through him. His chest squeezed. "What is it?"

"Joey has testicular cancer." Her voice crumbled as tears rolled down her cheeks, her shoulders shaking.

Chas's mind began to spin. "What? Are you sure?"

She barked out a hard laugh. "Of course I'm sure! He just told me."

He tried to digest the information. "Okay, well, can he get treatments for it?"

"He has no job, hence no medical insurance." She gulped, placing a hand over her mouth. "I'm sorry, I don't mean to burden you with this. I just wanted you to know what's going on." Her eyes met his for one long, terrible moment. "Why we can't see each other anymore."

The breath whooshed out of his lungs, a wave of dizziness rolling over him. "What? I don't understand."

She stared unseeingly ahead and began speaking dispassionately as if she were in a daze. "Joey will have to move in with me. I'll find a way to pay for his treatments and will take care of him."

A hard laugh rattled through his lips. "What? That's ridiculous. Joey's not your responsibility."

She spun around, eyes blazing. "Of course, he is! He's the father of my child!"

Chas's brows creased. "Yes, he is Noah's father, but he's not your husband."

The lines around her mouth tightened as she folded her arms over her chest. She was sitting next to him, but he got the sickening feeling that she was out of his reach. His mind raced for a solution. "Are you sure Joey has cancer? Maybe you should go with him to see a doctor, get a few different opinions, before you jump to conclusions."

She flinched, blinking rapidly. Her voice raised an octave. "Are you saying I'm lying?"

He fought to keep his voice even. "No, but what if Joey is?" An image of Joey flashed through his mind—surly, belligerent, willing to stoop to any level to get what he wanted. *I always win.* That's what Joey had said. Was this a Hail Mary to keep Ryleigh in his clutches? Even as the thoughts raced through his mind, he felt guilty. Cancer was a horrible thing. Chas wouldn't wish it on his worst enemy, not even Joey.

She rubbed her forehead, sounding weary. "Joey has an appointment with his oncologist tomorrow. I'm going with him."

"That's a good idea. Then you'll have all the facts." He raked a hand through his hair, trying to come up with a solution that would keep him from losing Ryleigh. Seeing her so broken was killing him inside. "How can I help?"

She flinched. "What?" she asked, her eyes rounding. Then a shadow overtook her features, and he had the impression she was sinking into a dark, fathomless pit. A pit so deep that no one, not even Chas could save her.

"I'd like to help." His mind clicked through the process—radiation, chemo. It would most likely be a long, expensive road. No way could Ryleigh shoulder this on her own. He couldn't believe he was even considering what he was about to say, but sitting here looking at Ryleigh, he couldn't see any other alternative. He loved Ryleigh. Now that he'd finally found her, he didn't want to let her go without a fight. "I'll pay for the treatments," he blurted.

She looked at him like he had two heads. "This is not your problem," she muttered, rocking back.

He touched her arm. "Anything that involves you, involves me." He squared his jaw, ready to field any argument she could throw at him. "I'll even pay for Joey's apartment." He didn't want Joey living with Ryleigh.

She leaned forward and rubbed both hands over her forehead and around her eyes.

"I can help."

She sat back up, glaring at him. He was taken aback at the vehemence in her eyes. Why had he suddenly become the enemy? "This isn't about the money," she heaved through tight lips.

The corners of his jaws twitched. "I beg to differ. It takes money to fight cancer."

She threw back her head, nostrils flaring. "Contrary to what you and your family believe, you can't just write a check and expect this to go away."

For a second, he was at a loss for words. "Where is this animosity coming from? Why're you dissing on my family? They've been nothing but kind to you."

She grunted. "You just don't understand." Her words rang with futility. "How could you? We come from two different worlds."

He tensed. "How so?"

She threw up her hands. "Your mother gave me a Prada bag that according to her had been 'laying around collecting dust.'" She made air quotes with her fingers. "She gave the handbags to her girlfriends as a party favor at a luncheon." She shook her head. "Who does that?" Her eyes held condemnation. "You could never understand what it was like to grow up without dependable parents."

The hair on the back of his neck rose. "You speak as though it's your kind against my kind, which, frankly, is a load of crap!"

Intensity shook her voice. "We are different! I have to work hard for every penny I earn, knowing that if I don't earn it, I won't have a roof over my head or food for my son. If you don't make it, you can just go home to your mansion and perfect family." Her jaw worked. "I need to be there one hundred percent for Joey. I can't just toss him aside for some romantic interlude."

Her words cut so deeply that for a second, he couldn't think straight. Then came the hot anger coursing like vinegar through his veins. "Don't presume that because you spent a weekend with my family that you know everything about them."

"Don't I?" she flung back, glaring at him.

"You think because you've had it hard that you're the only one who knows anything?" His spine stiffened. "Contrary to what you think, life hasn't been all wine and roses for me or my family. Do you know why my mom hosted that particular luncheon for her friends?"

Hesitation crept into her eyes.

"Do you?" he roared.

She flinched, her voice sounding small. "No."

"My mom has fibromyalgia. There are days when the pain is so bad that she can't even get out of bed." He punched out the words. "Those girlfriends you referred to have been there for my mom through thick and thin. That's why she bought them the bags. I'm sure she just told you the bit about the bag collecting dust, so her gift wouldn't make you uncomfortable."

Her eyes misted. "I didn't know," she squeaked.

The freight train had left the station and was raging full force now with Chas hardly hearing her response as he charged on. "Colin is not my oldest brother. I had another brother Griffin named after my dad. He died when he was three from a cancerous tumor. To this day, my mom still cries on Griffin's birthday." His voice shook with fury. "Colin and his wife got divorced because she wanted children and couldn't have them. They went through fertility treatments. She was pregnant three times with three miscarriages. After that, she had a mental breakdown." His voice caught. "So, don't tell me that my family doesn't know anything about pain and suffering!"

"I'm sorry." Tears rolled down her face.

He hated seeing her broken and distraught, hated knowing that his angry words had made the situation worse. His shoulders sagged. "I'm sorry about Joey, I really am. But this isn't really about Joey."

Her eyes flashed. "Of course it is. It's about loyalty. How could I look my son in the eyes, knowing I didn't do everything in my power to take care of his dad?"

"I just offered you a way to take care of Joey, but you're too stubborn to take it."

She squared her jaw, glaring at him.

He pushed out a hard laugh. "See? You know it's true and don't even bother denying it." He felt sick to his stomach, acid rising in his throat. A memory surfaced, rolling off his tongue, almost of its own accord. "My dad tells the story of a homeless man named Junior who would stand outside the doors of the sporting goods store and beg for money. 'You got any spare change you can part with?' Junior would say in a slow, garbled tone to everyone who passed by. One day, my dad decided to make Junior's day. When Junior asked for change, Dad slapped a twenty-dollar bill in his hand. Junior looked at it with a blank expression then the rote words tumbled out of his mouth. 'You got any spare change to go with that?'"

He let out a heavy breath. "You're just like Junior. You hold my heart in the palms of your hands and yet for you it's just spare change. A romantic interlude." Hurt sliced like a knife through his gut. "For me, it's everything." He balled a fist and put it to his mouth. He'd thought his love could overcome anything. He'd been a fool.

Sobs wrenched her throat. She put a hand over her mouth to stifle them, her shoulders heaving.

"I'm sorry I've made you cry," he said flatly. "Above all, I wish you could see the confident, incredible woman that I see when I look at you." A deep sadness rankled his gut. "At the end of the day, it doesn't matter how I see you." He paused. "What matters is how you see yourself."

She stumbled to her feet. "I'm sorry," she stammered as she fled the room. A minute later, he heard the front door open and close.

A curious numbness settled over him. Had he really lost her? Tears gathered in his eyes, his gut twisting. Finally, he stood, his feet heavy as he went into the kitchen and picked up his phone. "Hey, McKenna it's me, Chas. Can you do me a favor? There's a man named Joey Martin—Ryleigh's ex-husband. I need you to look into him for me."

18

The next twenty-four hours were some of the most painful of her life. Ryleigh cried until there were no tears left. Chas was right about the things he'd said. She had misjudged him and his family. She felt like a louse about it, but it still didn't change the fact that she had to stand by Joey's side. She'd stayed up half the night, researching treatments for testicular cancer. She had no idea how she was going to shoulder this. Hopefully, Joey's family could help. After they met with the oncologist, she was going to suggest gathering Joey's family to come up with a plan. They were good, reasonable people. Ryleigh felt sure they'd help.

Maybe she should've let Chas help. She cradled her head in her hands, massaging her temples. She'd felt like a zombie this morning as she got up and helped Noah get ready for school. Tess had left early, saying she had a few errands to run, but Ryleigh knew the real reason Tess had left. She was ticked because Joey had moved into the spare bedroom the night before. Tess told Ryleigh that it was a mistake to let him come back. "You should've let him go to his parent's house instead," Tess said. "What kind of mixed message will this send to Noah?"

All the hurt and anger had boiled to a head as Ryleigh got up in

Tess's face. "Noah will know that his mother is kind and compassionate. That when things got tough, I didn't desert his father like Mom did us."

Tess didn't back down an inch. "This isn't about what Mom did. The situation is different. You and Joey are divorced. Cancer or not. Joey is a slime ball!"

Around and around they went until the argument ended in a frigid silence.

Ryleigh had rescheduled all her appointments for today. She should be working but she was frozen, unable to think, much less do. It was all she could do to get Noah off to school. Then she came into the kitchen and washed down a piece of toast with a glass of water. Even that made her nauseated. Her thoughts went back to Chas. The feeling of loss that ran through her was so swift that it nearly stole her breath away. It had been cruel and insensitive to label what they had as a *romantic interlude*. She hadn't meant it. She was angry and frustrated, wanting to lash out. Chas must think she was a horrible person. Tears rose in her eyes. Like he said, his family had been nothing but kind to her, and she'd wrongfully judged them. His words about confidence burned through her mind. She knew she lacked confidence. It was something she constantly worked on. She thought she was doing better, but obviously not.

Hands slipped over her shoulders, massaging them. She jerked, whirling around, shocked to see Joey standing before her in nothing but boxer shorts.

She straightened in her seat, glaring at him. "What do you think you're doing?"

A friendly smile stole over his lips. "You seemed tense. I was just trying to help."

"Well, don't!" she snapped. Then she felt guilty. He looked pathetic with his head shaved. He said that he decided to part with the hair now rather than waiting until chemotherapy.

He held up his hands. "You're right. I'm sorry." He lowered his head in surrender. "My bad." He scratched his chest as he went to the refrigerator and retrieved a carton of orange juice. He grabbed a tall glass out of the cabinet and filled it, downing it in a few gulps. Then, he sat the glass down on the counter with a loud plunk. "Thanks for letting me sleep in. I didn't even hear you and Noah leave this morning."

"No worries. I'm sure you need the extra rest." It was eleven am, and Ryleigh was still sitting here like a knot on a log. Who was she to judge?

He gave her a searching look. "I'm so sorry about all this."

"It's not your fault," she said rhetorically. "Cancer's not something you ever see coming."

"No, it's not." He walked around the table and pulled out a chair, sitting down across from her. "I appreciate you letting me stay here. I would've stayed with my parents, but their place is so small … It's just temporary, until I can get through the treatments."

She exhaled, gathering her thoughts. "Joey, I'll help any way I can, but I don't have the money to pay for all of your treatments."

He reached for her hand. "I know, babe. I don't expect you to do that."

"What do you mean?" She removed her hand.

"I spoke to my parents. They have some money saved up and offered to help."

Relief surged through her. "That would be great," she breathed. "After we meet with the oncologist this afternoon, we should stop by and talk to your parents."

He rubbed a hand over his head. "Uh, about the meeting with the oncologist."

She frowned. "Yes?"

"Dr. Tinley's nurse called this morning. The poor doc is down for the count with the flu. We won't be able to meet with him until next week."

Her heart lurched. "Isn't there someone else we could meet with? One of his partners, maybe?"

"I trust Dr. Tinley. I'd rather wait for him."

"But every day that you wait could increase the chance of the cancer spreading."

"True," he conceded, "even so, I feel better about waiting."

A few more days wouldn't be the end of the world, but it felt like the end. Ryleigh wanted to get a clear picture of what Joey was dealing with, so they'd know the best way to fight it.

Tess burst into the kitchen, her jaw set in a determined stance. She shot Joey a scathing look before dropping an envelope in front of Ryleigh. Ryleigh turned it over, realized it wasn't sealed. "What is this?"

Tess pulled out a chair with a loud scrape and plopped down. "See for yourself," she ordered.

Ryleigh pulled out the contents and opened the paper. Tears sprang to her eyes when she realized it was from Chas. She gasped when she saw the cashier's check. Her hand trembled as she picked it up and read the amount. Two hundred and ten thousand dollars. The check dropped from her hand as she reached for the note.

Ryleigh,

The ten thousand is the payment I promised for the party. Use the other amount for Joey's treatments ... or anything else that you need. Please know that taking this money in no way obligates you to me. I simply want to help. You owe me that much.

Chas

She traced over the letters of his name with the tip of her finger, tears glistening in her eyes. She turned to Tess. "Did you see Chas?" The longing for him was nearly unbearable. Her life felt dead and empty without him. For the first time, she understood why her dad had been so broken. She clutched her fist. She couldn't think this way. She had Noah to look after. She owed it to her son to do all she could to help Joey. Once Joey was cured, she'd be free of him.

"No, I went to visit Gemma," Tess answered. "Chas had stopped by earlier to give her this, knowing either you or I would eventually stop by."

A tear escaped, dribbling down Ryleigh's cheek. Before she could stop him, Joey reached for the check, his eyes bulging. "Wow," he uttered with a low whistle. "This is a lot of moolah."

"Give me that," Tess growled, snatching it from his hands.

"Hey, watch it! You'll rip it," Joey said. His eyes moved to Ryleigh. "Lover boy must be gaga over you."

The sneer in his tone caused Ryleigh's blood pressure to spike. "Yes, he loves me as I love him. He gave me the money to help relieve the stress that he knows will be caused by your treatments." She heard the accusation in her own voice, knew it wasn't right to resent Joey. Still, it was how she felt right now. She hated cancer and the havoc it wreaked on families.

"I think you should take the money," Joey said.

"I agree," Tess added. She held up the check. "This will help pay for Joey's treatments." She shot him a look laced with malice. "You could even put him up in his own apartment with this kind of money. Get him the heck out of here."

Joey's eyes rounded as he gave Ryleigh a pleading look. "Who'll take care of me?" The plaintive note in his voice caused Ryleigh to soften.

"We're not throwing Joey out, and we're not taking the money," Ryleigh said.

Joey's jaw went slack. "Why not?"

Ryleigh gritted her teeth. "Because it's too much. I won't take advantage of Chas's generosity that way."

Tess shook her head. "You're making a big mistake." Her voice lowered to a hiss. "There's no way you can afford to pay for Joey's treatments. We're barely making ends meet as it is."

"Joey's parents agreed to help with the treatments," Ryleigh said. She felt like she was in deep water, about to go under, and grasping for a life preserver.

Joey laughed uneasily. "Yeah, they did, but it'll exhaust their life savings. Now, that's not necessary since he's willing to foot the bill."

The callous way Joey threw out the words got under Ryleigh's skin. Tears burned her eyes. "I know you can't help that you have cancer, but do you have any idea what this has cost me or Chas? Do you!" she yelled when Joey remained silent. "I love Chas." Her lower lip trembled, tears streaming down her cheeks. "We were going to build a future together."

Joey gave her a look of pity as he slowly shook his head back and forth. "It was a nice dream, babe, but it never would've worked. You and Mr. Superstar are from two different worlds. His kind doesn't mix with our kind."

Ryleigh's head jerked. "What did you say?" How long had Joey been planting those seeds of doubt in her head? Maybe he'd started doing it when he realized those were her weakest points. When did she start listening to him? The truth of Chas's words hit her full force.

"You and I both know that the thing with Chas would've fizzled out when the next pretty thing came along," Joey continued.

"You scumbag!" Tess seethed. "Cancer or not, I ought to wring your neck!"

"You'll have to get in line behind me," Ryleigh said through clenched teeth.

Joey's eyes darted back and forth as he laughed nervously. "Wait a minute, ladies. Don't get your panties in a wad. I'm just speaking practically. Two hundred and ten thou is nothing to sneer at." His eyes lit with avarice. "Think about all that we could do with that kind of money."

"Like pay for your cancer treatments?" Tess fired.

"Yeah, that and more," Joey said.

"Since when did this become a *we* situation?" Ryleigh pressed.

Joey's face flushed, emphasizing the pale sheen of his head.

It was crazy how in that moment, everything became clear like a lens of a camera coming into focus. "I will take the money."

A goofy grin spilled over Joey's lips. "Smart girl," he beamed.

Tess looked relieved.

Ryleigh sat up straight in her seat. "You're Noah's father. Because of Noah, I will use that money to pay for your cancer treatments ... and to rent you an apartment."

Joey's face fell.

"Hallelujah," Tess muttered. "Finally, you're starting to make some sense."

"Yes," Ryleigh agreed, hope sprouting in her breast. "It's about time I came to my senses." She leveled a glare at Joey. "I love Chas, and I want to build a life with him."

"What're you saying?" Joey's face twisted with anger.

Ryleigh lifted her chin. "I'm saying that I've spent far too long devaluing my worth, and it's time that I stopped." She wanted to jump up this instant and run to Chas, beg his forgiveness.

Tess's eyes shone with tears. "Yes," she exclaimed jubilantly. "You finally see it!"

Accusation sounded in Joey's voice. "What about my cancer?"

"Like I said, I'll use the money to make sure that you get your treatments," Ryleigh said. "That's more than fair, considering the two of us are divorced and have been for years."

"While you float off into the sunset with Mr. Perfect?" Joey taunted. "That hardly seems fair."

"Life is rarely fair," Tess countered. "If it were, we wouldn't be sitting here having this conversation." Her phone rang. "Excuse me," she said, "I need to take this." Tess got up, taking the check with her as she walked into the other room.

Joey's expression was sullen. "So, that's how it's gonna be, huh? You're choosing him over me."

"Joey, that choice was made a long time ago when we got divorced."

"I never stopped loving you." His voice caught. "I had hoped that you might feel the same way."

"What you need to focus on right now is getting well. You owe that to Noah."

He cursed under his breath.

Tess stormed back into the room like a raging bull. "I just got off the phone with Henrietta."

Joey's face grew chalky. "You called my mother?"

"Yes, I did. I tried to call your sister Natalie, but she's on a cruise. So, I did the next best thing and called Henrietta."

"What's going on?" Ryleigh asked.

"Joey doesn't have cancer," Tess spat. "He's perfectly healthy. You know how I said he looked puny that day in the office? Well, that was because he'd just gotten over the stomach flu."

Trembles started in Ryleigh's hands, going down to her toes. "What?" She felt like her spirit had been severed from her body and that she was watching the events unfold from afar. She looked at Joey, could tell from the guilty look in his eyes that he'd been caught. Her head felt like it was on fire. "How could you?" Anger crowded out all reason as she jumped to her feet, tears stinging her eyes. "You set me up!"

"You low-down snake!" Tess's voice grew musing. "Did you think we wouldn't find out?"

Joey rose to his feet. "Of course I knew you'd find out," he blustered. "I was just buying time." He shot Tess an accusing look. "You're the one who gave me the idea, jabbering about how sick I looked."

Tess's voice rose. "Oh, no. Don't you go blaming your actions on me! That was all on you!"

"You said you were buying time. Time for what?" The words shot like bullets out of Ryleigh's mouth.

"Time to get that creep out of your life. I did what I had to, to protect what's mine." He thrust out his chest.

"Get out!" Ryleigh shouted.

He growled out a surly laugh. "Are you kicking me out? Really?"

"You heard her," Tess said holding up the phone. "Get out before I call the police!"

"Fine. I'll leave." He shot Ryleigh a condemning look. "You'll regret this."

"I already regret the time I wasted on you."

"I'm still Noah's father." A cruel smile curled his lips. "I can make your life very difficult."

"You already have," Ryleigh answered realizing that'd she'd finally broken free of Joey's control. It was liberating.

He laughed, then cursed as he stomped out of the kitchen.

Ryleigh's hand went to her chest. It was too much for her body to handle. The stress of the cancer, then finding out there was no cancer. She was relieved, yet fighting mad at Joey. Chas had questioned if Joey really had cancer, and she'd been angry with him because of it. "I've got to go to Chas, tell him what a huge mistake I made."

Tess's lips turned down. "I'm afraid that's not possible."

Panic seized Ryleigh. "Why not?"

"Gemma told me that Chas left for New Orleans right after he dropped off the envelope. He said he needed to get away for a few days and clear his head. He isn't coming back until the day of the Bachelor Auction."

Ryleigh's knees gave way as she slumped down in a chair. "I've ruined everything." Iron bands wrapped around her chest, making it hard to breathe.

Tess put a hand on her shoulder. "Don't panic. There has to be a way to get him back."

"You think so?" Ryleigh gulped. Her head was spinning so fast she feared she might black out.

"Yeah, we'll think of something," Tess answered. Her eyes sparked. "But first, let's make sure that Bozo gets his junk packed and gets out of here."

19

The Rosecrest Mansion was impressive on a normal basis. However, tonight, amidst the excitement of the Bachelor Auction, the luxury hotel gleamed like a prized jewel against the indigo sky. Ryleigh clutched her Prada bag, taking in a deep breath, willing herself to remain calm. She pushed her way past the throngs of photographers snapping pictures of everything that moved. Everyone waited on bated breath for the bachelors to arrive.

Ryleigh showed her ticket to the doorman, then proceeded through a security station that included a metal detector. She hurried into the foyer, wanting to make sure she got into the hotel before Chas arrived and saw her. She looked around at the scores of beautiful, pampered women, all waiting to get their shot at bidding on five Titans' players, Chas included. For a split second, Ryleigh had the impulse to flee back home as fast as she could. She could talk to Chas later. Even as the thought flitted through her mind, she straightened her shoulders. No, she had to face this. Her need for Chas was greater than her fears, greater than her weaknesses. The last few days without Chas had been pure agony. She couldn't take another minute away from him. She rubbed a hand against the soft silk of her emerald dress, sucking in her stomach.

She'd gone to great lengths to get here tonight. Gemma had pulled some strings and managed to get her a five-thousand-dollar ticket. Then, Gemma, Tess, and Ryleigh went shopping for the perfect dress. It had taken them an entire day and eighteen hundred dollars to get her outfitted. All of this came from the money that Chas had given her for Joey's supposed treatments. Tess wanted Ryleigh to get her hair done, but Ryleigh decided to fix it herself. She was already so made up that she hardly recognized herself. If she did too much to herself, Chas might not recognize her. She smiled at the thought, knowing she was being overly dramatic.

Ryleigh had just over two hundred and three thousand dollars left, and she was prepared to spend every cent of that on Chas. Hopefully, it would be enough. She wanted Chas to know in a big way that she was all in. She had a lot of making up to do. The auction would be the first step. Her biggest fear, the one that had kept her up at night all week, was that Chas might not want her anymore. She'd said some hurtful things, and he'd been blunt with her too. She had been like the homeless man outside the sporting goods store. For so many years she'd believed that she wasn't worthy of true happiness, so she'd settled for *spare change*. Not anymore!

As she stepped into the large banquet room, a sense of awe swept over her. The place was magnificent. Her pulse pounded in her ears as she made her way over to a table. There were several tables reserved in the front, but the majority looked to be first come, first served. She'd just scouted out a spot and was making her way over to it when someone touched her arm. She was jolted at the sight of Selena Simpson. The diva wore a black sequin dress that showcased her mile-long legs. Her hair was swept up in a chic twist, that made her look even taller. It was a good thing Ryleigh was wearing heels, or else she would've felt like a dwarf in comparison.

Selena looked her up and down with a disapproving eye. "You're that chef," she said, her full lips forming a pout.

"Yes, I am," Ryleigh said proudly in such a forthright tone that it cowed Selena a little. However, it only took a second for the woman to gather her wits and sling a verbal barb.

"If you're looking for the kitchen, you're in the wrong place." Her haughty expression was so caustic that it dissolved all her beauty. There were so many things Ryleigh could've said to put this woman in her place. No longer would she be quelled by Selena or anyone like her.

A velvety laugh trilled from Ryleigh's throat as she flicked her hair like Tess often did. "Don't you wish I was here for the kitchen," she taunted.

Selena's face fell. "Why are you here?"

"I think you already know the answer to that," she said lightly as she sauntered away like she was the Queen of Sheba. "Take that, you horrible debutante," she muttered, feeling a burst of triumph. She sat down at an open spot and crossed her legs, adjusting her dress. *Just breathe, Ryleigh.* Her phone buzzed. It was a text from Tess saying, *You've got this.* She looked down, uttering a silent prayer as she clutched the handbag.

Surprisingly, Effie's handbag helped bolster her courage, reminding Ryleigh of all that she and Chas had experienced together. Surely, he'd forgive her.

The room began to fill as women of all ages settled in around her, chattering like clucking chickens. A rumble went through the crowd when Scarlett Lily, a well-known actress took the stage. With her lively, blue eyes and long, red hair, she reminded Ryleigh of McKenna, Chas's sister. "Ladies," Scarlett gushed in a juicy tone, "are you ready to have some fun?"

Applause broke out.

"Five lucky ladies will get to spend Valentine's Day with a hunky Titans' player. Just a reminder, all proceeds from tonight will go to benefit Little Lambs, a foster care program." Scarlett pumped a large smile. "So, be generous." She waved an arm. "All right, bring out the bachelors." Music played in the background as the Titans emerged from the side stage. Women all around Ryleigh jumped to their feet and cheered like they were at a rock concert. The men were all attractive, but her eyes gravitated towards Chas, her heart catching in her throat. His blue, button-down shirt and charcoal slacks were noticeably casual compared to his teammates. He had the same confident set in his shoulders and step that was so Chas, but his smile was strained like he'd rather be anywhere than here.

The Titans took their seats, facing the crowd.

Scarlett Lily chirped on with a few jokes, but Ryleigh hardly heard a word. She glanced at the paddle on the table, mentally preparing herself for the bidding. She didn't know what she would do if someone outbid her. Her heart lurched as a fear seized her. What if Selena Simpson won the bid? She shut off the negative thoughts. *Think positively*, she ordered herself.

An army of waiters dressed in black tuxedos placed Waldorf salads in front of each lady. It looked good, but Ryleigh was too keyed up to eat. She stirred the food around for a bit, taking a bite. Then, she placed her fork down, unable to eat any more. She followed a similar pattern when the entrees of prime rib and salmon were served. Her eyes were glued to Chas as he made conversation with the two players sitting on either side of him. She was so drawn to him that she wondered if he might feel her presence in the room.

The dinner seemed to take forever to wind down. Just when Ryleigh didn't think she could take another moment of anticipation, Scarlett emerged. As if on cue, the waiters began removing the empty plates.

One of the Titans' players sprang up, hopped off the stage, and darted through the room like he was chasing after someone. Murmurs rustled through the crowd as a lady dressed in a silver sequin dress went after him.

The bidding started with the player on the far left. The numbers climbed high quickly as paddles shot up around the room. Ryleigh's mind was in such a state that she couldn't even remember the amount the first Titan went for.

When it was Chas's turn, Ryleigh's heart pounded so fiercely that she thought it might burst out of her chest. Chas took the stage, smiling and waving.

"The casual look works well on you," Scarlett said.

"Thanks," Chas responded in an offhanded manner like he

couldn't care less what Scarlett Lily or the other women in the room thought of him. A smile tugged at Ryleigh's lips. *That's my man.*

"All right ladies, it's the Irish Flash."

Whistles sounded across the room.

"How about we start the bidding at twenty-five grand?" A paddle went up in the front. "Who'll give me thirty?" Several other paddles went up. Ryleigh clutched the paddle stick with tight knuckles. The price kept steadily rising. "One hundred grand," Scarlett boomed. "Remember, it's for charity. Who'll make it more?" Another paddle went up.

Ryleigh's chest squeezed as she gulped in a breath. She was so keyed up she was dizzy.

The price was now at one hundred and fifty. "One hundred fifty-five."

Ryleigh's heart nearly stopped when she spotted Selena a handful of tables away. "One hundred sixty-five," Selena said loudly, holding up her paddle as she gave Chas a hopeful smile.

"Do I hear one hundred seventy?" Scarlett asked.

Silence.

Ryleigh swallowed. *Now or never!* She hoped Chas would forgive her for spending his money. At least it was for charity.

"One hundred seventy, going once."

Ryleigh thrust her paddle high in the air. "Two hundred thousand," she said loudly as all eyes turned to her. The room shrank, and all Ryleigh could see was Chas. The look of shock on his handsome face was almost comical, making her want to break down giggling hysterically. She swallowed the ridiculous urge, straightening her shoulders.

Scarlett laughed. "All right. Now we're talking. Two hundred thousand. Do I hear two hundred five?"

Ryleigh's jaw clenched, hoping against hope that she'd win the bid.

"Two hundred thousand going once."

Ryleigh held her breath, squeezing so hard on the paddle that she broke the stick. The pop made her jump slightly.

"Going twice. Sold for two hundred thousand."

The air whooshed out of Ryleigh's lungs as her knees wobbled. Even from this distance, Chas's eyes burned into hers. Then a lopsided grin tugged at one corner of his lips. She felt herself smile back. The bidding continued as Chas left the stage and returned to his seat. Realizing she was still standing, she sat down.

"Congratulations," the woman next to her said. She shook her head. "You must've wanted him bad."

"You have no idea," Ryleigh murmured.

After the auction was over, Ryleigh sifted through the crowd, making her way towards the stage. Her heart dropped when she realized Chas's seat was empty. She looked around, not seeing him. She swallowed, trying to loosen the tightness in her throat. It had never occurred to her that Chas might leave after she won the bid. Her eyes misted, her heart pounding dully against her ribcage like a deflated ball. Had she lost him?

She felt a tug on her hand. "Hello," Chas said as he turned her around to face him.

"Hello," she repeated, blinking back the tears.

"What was that?" Chas asked, searching her face.

"An apology," she croaked, then coughed to clear her throat.

An enigmatic expression overtook his rugged features as he took hold of her hand. "Come with me." He pulled her up the side stairs and to the back of the stage. When they were in a secluded corner, he turned to face her. His eyes deepened with intensity as they moved over her. "You look incredible."

She smiled. "I'm glad you like it. You paid for it ... with the money you gave me."

He chuckled. "I suspect that I also paid handsomely for our Valentine's date just now."

Color rose in her cheeks. "Yes, I'm afraid so."

His expression remained guarded, making it impossible to gauge his emotions. Her mind raced for something to fill the silence. "You look nice too." She touched his shirt. "Although you seem to be a bit underdressed," she teased, giving him a partial smile, hoping to ease some of the tension between them. "Did you come straight from the airport?"

"Yep, my luggage is still in the car."

She moistened her lips, needing to get everything out in one fell swoop. "I'm sorry about the things I said. I had no right to judge you or your family." Her voice trembled, but she pressed on. "You were right about Joey. The cancer was a sham to get me back."

His eyes widened, then narrowed. "I'm not surprised. McKenna has been doing some digging. She hasn't discovered that yet, but she's found out a few other unsavory things. How Joey was fired from one of his jobs for selling company secrets. How he mouthed off to one of his bosses and then punched the sixty-year-old man."

"You got McKenna to investigate?"

"Yep." He squared his chin like he was ready to defend himself.

Ryleigh's jaw tightened. "At this point, there's nothing you could tell me about Joey that would surprise me. For the record, I chose you even before I realized Joey was lying about the cancer."

Surprise flashed in his eyes.

Emotion rose in her throat. "And, you were right about the confidence. I do need to change my thought processes." A smile flitted over her lips. "Unfortunately, the slow phase of the learning is a real kick in the pants. Still, I'm trying."

He grunted out a laugh. "Practice makes perfect."

She stepped closer, cupping his jaw. "Chas, these past few days away from you have been torture."

"Good."

She flinched, giving him a questioning look.

A crooked grin slid over his lips. "Because they've been brutal for me too."

She laughed, catching the full meaning of his words. He slid his arms around her waist, pulling her close. Her breath came faster as he lowered his head, gazing into her eyes. "You paid a lot of money for me tonight," he murmured.

"No, you paid a lot of money."

His eyes lit with pleasure. "The money was yours to do with as you wished, remember?"

A grin stole over her lips. "I spent the money exactly as I should have," she said fiercely. "The best purchase I've ever made."

His rich laughter filled the space between them. "You can't imagine the thoughts that were running through my head when I was on the stage. I heard your voice, saw you standing back there like an angel. It was all I could do not to charge off the stage and scoop you up in my arms."

Tears glittered in her eyes. "Thank you for being so wonderful." Sheer happiness bubbled inside her as she soaked in the lines of his handsome face. Her heart expanded, yearning to give voice to all that she was feeling. "I love you, Chas O'Brien."

He blinked. "You do?"

"Yes," she exclaimed joyously, laughing and crying at the same time.

He chuckled. "Aren't you jumping the gun? What about the four-month rule?"

A grin slid over her lips. "Hang the four-month rule. What's four months in comparison to the real deal?"

"Amen," he uttered as his lips took hers in a long, thorough kiss that sent quivers of desire trembling through her.

Bits of her life shifted before her like a kaleidoscope. All her life, her heart had been on a long, twisty journey, but she'd finally found home.

Chas O'Brien had done what no one else could do.

He'd taken the impossible and made it possible.

EPILOGUE

Ryleigh mentally ran through all the steps she'd go through during the next two hours. She turned to Tess. "Be sure and check on Noah." She chuckled. "Or rather Gemma and Doug. It was nice of them to watch Noah today during the competition."

Tess chomped on her gum. "All right. Will do," she said absently, clenching and unclenching her hands as she glanced towards the cavernous room that housed the work stations for the cooking competition participants. "You have two hours to prepare both dishes. That should be more than enough time ... as long as you don't panic."

Ryleigh laughed. "It's not me I'm worried about. You're jumpier than a grasshopper hyped up on sugar."

Tess fanned her face. "Yeah, this is a bit stressful."

"Nah, all in a day's work," Ryleigh said easily with a wave of her hand. She looked at Chas, who flashed an encouraging smile.

"You've got this. Your salmon and shrimp are phenomenal." His eyes moved over hers in that slow leisurely way that made her go weak in the knees. "You look fantastic too. How could everyone not love you?" A lock of hair slid over one eye as he flashed a boyish grin that shot a dart of warmth through her. "I sure love you."

Her heart sang with delight. "I love you too," she uttered, lifting her lips to give him a quick kiss. With Chas by her side, there was nothing Ryleigh couldn't do. She'd been walking on air ever since the night of the auction. At this rate, she might never come back down to earth.

"Ugh!" Tess squawked, but her eyes were dancing. She gulped in a breath, the words rushing out breathlessly. "Do you remember all the ingredients for the peanut butter pie? How to dress it up so that it looks gourmet?"

Ryleigh tapped her temple. "A steel trap." There was a full-fledged grocery store set up inside the competition area. The ten contestants had twenty minutes to gather ingredients before starting the food prep. Ryleigh had deliberated over what to prepare and then decided to make the dishes that she knew best. If Chas had taught her anything, it was that she was enough. She didn't need to devalue herself or her skills.

"All contestants please report to their stations," an announcer said over the loudspeaker.

Tess rubbed her hands together. "Showtime, sis." Her voice tingled with excitement. "You've got what it takes to win this."

A surge of happiness went through Ryleigh as she locked eyes with Chas. "I'm already a winner!"

"Yes, you are." He winked. "Now, go get 'em."

YOUR FREE BOOK AWAITS ...

Hey there, thanks for taking the time to read *The Impossible Groom*. If you enjoyed it, please take a minute to give me a review on Amazon. I really appreciate your feedback, as I depend largely on word of mouth to promote my books.

To receive updates when more of my books are coming out, sign up for my newsletter at http://jenniferyoungblood.com/

If you sign up for my newsletter, I'll give you one of my books, Beastly Charm: A contemporary retelling of beauty & the beast, for FREE. Plus, you'll get information on discounts and other freebies. For more information, visit:

http://bit.ly/freebookjenniferyoungblood

Your Free Book Awaits ...

BOOKS BY JENNIFER YOUNGBLOOD

Check out Jennifer's Amazon Page:
http://bit.ly/jenniferyoungblood

Georgia Patriots Romance
The Hot Headed Patriot
The Twelfth Hour Patriot

O'Brien Family Romance
The Impossible Groom (Chas O'Brien)
The Twelfth Hour Patriot (McKenna O'Brien)
Rewriting Christmas (A Novella)
Yours By Christmas (Park City Firefighter Romance)
Her Crazy Rich Fake Fiancé

Navy SEAL Romance
The Resolved Warrior
The Reckless Warrior
The Diehard Warrior
Get the Navy SEAL Romance Collection

The Jane Austen Pact
  Seeking Mr. Perfect
  Get the Christmas Romance Collection

Texas Titan Romances
  The Hometown Groom
  The Persistent Groom
  The Ghost Groom
  The Jilted Billionaire Groom
  The Impossible Groom
  Get the Texas Titan Romance Collection
  The Perfect Catch (Last Play Series)

Hawaii Billionaire Series
  Love Him or Lose Him
  Love on the Rocks
  Love on the Rebound
  Love at the Ocean Breeze
  Love Changes Everything
  Loving the Movie Star
  Love Under Fire (A Companion book to the Hawaii Billionaire Series)
  Get the entire Hawaii Billionaire Romance Collection

Kisses and Commitment Series
  How to See With Your Heart

Angel Matchmaker Series
  Kisses Over Candlelight
  The Cowboy and the Billionaire's Daughter
  Get the Heart and Soul Collection

Romantic Thrillers
  False Identity
  False Trust

Promise Me Love
Burned
Get the entire Romance Suspense Collection

Contemporary Romance
Beastly Charm

Fairytale Retellings (The Grimm Laws Series)
Banish My Heart **(This book is FREE)**
The Magic in Me
Under Your Spell
A Love So True

Southern Romance
Livin' in High Cotton
Recipe for Love
Get the entire Southern Romance Collection

The Second Chance Series
Forgive Me (Book 1)
Love Me (Book 2)

Short Stories
The Southern Fried Fix

ABOUT JENNIFER YOUNGBLOOD

Jennifer loves reading and writing clean romance. She believes that happily ever after is not just for stories. Jennifer enjoys interior design, rollerblading, clogging, jogging, and chocolate. In Jennifer's opinion there are few ills that can't be solved with a warm brownie and scoop of vanilla-bean ice cream.

Jennifer grew up in rural Alabama and loved living in a town where "everybody knows everybody." Her love for writing began as a young teenager when she wrote stories for her high school English teacher to critique.

Jennifer has BA in English and Social Sciences from Brigham Young University where she served as Miss BYU Hawaii in 1989. Before becoming an author, she worked as the owner and editor of a monthly newspaper named *The Senior Times*.

She now lives in the Rocky Mountains with her family and spends her time writing and doing all of the wonderful things that make up the life of a busy wife and mother.

facebook.com/authorjenniferyoungblood
twitter.com/authorjenni
instagram.com/authorjenniferyoungblood

Copyright © 2019 by Jennifer Youngblood

All rights reserved.

No part of this collection may be reproduced in any form or by any electronic or mechanical means, including information storage and retrieval systems, without written permission from the author, except for the use of brief quotations in a book review.

Visit Jennifer's official website at

http://jenniferyoungblood.com

Made in the USA
Middletown, DE
13 July 2021